# that
# beautiful
# atlantic
# waltz

Also by Malachy Tallack

*Illuminated by Water*
*The Valley at the Centre of the World*
*The Un-Discovered Islands*
*60 Degrees North*

# that beautiful atlantic waltz

## Malachy Tallack

CANONGATE

First published in Great Britain, the USA and Canada in 2024
by Canongate Books Ltd, 14 High Street, Edinburgh EH1 1TE

Distributed in the USA by Publishers Group West and in Canada
by Publishers Group Canada

canongate.co.uk

1

*British Library Cataloguing-in-Publication Data*
A catalogue record for this book is available on
request from the British Library

ISBN 978 1 83885 498 0

Typeset in Bembo by Palimpsest Book Production Ltd,
Falkirk, Stirlingshire

Printed and bound by CPI Group (UK) Ltd, Croydon CR0 4YY

MIX
Paper | Supporting
responsible forestry
FSC® C171272
www.fsc.org

I am thinking tonight of an old cottage home
That stands on the brow of the hill
Where in life's early morning I once loved to roam
But now all is quiet and still

'My Old Cottage Home'

# the great wave

## 1957

A nd all at once, as though commanded into being, a great wave rose. It rose at first like the broad back of a whale, and then, like something monstrous, something mountainous, it rose higher still.

Those men who stood on the ship's bridge looked out upon the water, and they knew in that instant just how frail their vessel could be. For weeks, they had sailed the ice-clotted ocean, seeking and slaughtering the creatures of this place. They had left them, those giant bodies, to be flensed and rendered, to be translated into blubber and blood, into oil and meal, into lipstick and margarine. They had worked until their own bones shuddered with exhaustion, their skin puckered and split with cold. They had longed, these men, for their homes.

In storms past, they had found shelter, had huddled in the lee of icebergs, some as big as islands, others as big as cities. They had waited for the worst to pass, and then had gone to work again. But this storm was different. It came without warning, in the last week of the year. The wind had pawed and needled, then had struck them like a fist. The ship had rocked and groaned as the first waves came. But those were as nothing compared to what came next.

Most of the men aboard could not see the great wave – from their cabins, from the engine room, from the mess – but all seemed to know it was coming. Inside the ship, the air had thickened; nostrils, eyes and throats had clogged with salt. All senses turned towards the water.

As the wall of ocean began to crest above them, each man took hold of what seemed to him most solid. Some of them must have prayed, mouthing words they had not spoken since last in church. Others thought of wives and children, or the wives and children that they hoped one day to have. They thought of mothers and fathers and friends and lovers, and of the islands and the cities they had left behind.

And when the great wave fell finally upon them, when air became water and water became everything and everything was drenched in darkness, death seemed certain – the end, for all of them, decided. They closed their eyes and clenched their bodies, each believing they had few breaths left to breathe, few seconds still remaining.

And then, those seconds gone, another moment came, drenched in light, in which those men could wonder if perhaps their prayers had been answered, if perhaps the ship on which they stood might stay afloat, if perhaps – a miracle – each one of them would see his home again.

There were some amongst those men who felt in that bright moment, and in the hours that came afterwards, as though they had been reborn, as though the wave had washed them clean and thrown them out into the world again anew. None spoke this feeling aloud. All assumed that they alone had felt it, that they alone had been spared for a reason.

For one of those men – Sonny, a deckboy, just turned twenty, and on his third trip to the Southern Ocean – the reason was clear. When he returned to Shetland in five months' time, with the packet of cash in his pocket, and the smell of rancid oil and caustic soda embedded in his skin, he would ask Kathleen Anderson of Treswick to marry him. Sweet, honey-eyed Kathleen. And together they would make a home.

# 1

The Paton house, called Hamar, stood half a mile from the Atlantic shore, behind a jagged ridge of granite that obscured all views of the water. Tourists passing the spot in June might have wondered at this fact. Why build a house on an island from which the sea cannot be seen? But had those tourists come back again in winter, with a gale from the south-west howling, the answer would have been clear. The house lay in shelter. It faced the fields that once belonged to those who lived inside.

Jack Paton, who was now the sole occupant of Hamar, did not own those fields. He had sold the croft a few years after his parents died – both of them, together, in the summer he turned twenty-one – keeping only the house, the long stone shed, and a strip of garden between the two.

From a certain angle, Jack's house appeared, still, like the simple three-room cottage that for more than half a century it had been. From that certain angle, the ugly extension his father had built in 1960, the year Jack was born – the extra bedroom, the narrow kitchen, the chilly bathroom – were more or less invisible. But even then, the house could not be called pretty. It was too plain, too long from its last lick of paint for that.

For many years after Jack sold the croft, Hamar had stood alone, at the end of an unsurfaced track whose countless potholes needed to be filled and refilled every summer. Then, a decade ago, Jack's nearest neighbour, Old Andrew, who had bought the land from him, had a heart attack and retired. His eldest son – also Andrew – sold a plot of that land shortly afterwards, at the other end of the track where it met the main road. An English couple bought it and built a house: an enormous wooden thing, Swedish blue, with windows everywhere and a wide porch like something from a Western film. They lived there together for seven years, until the husband moved away, leaving behind his wife, Sarah, and young daughter, Vaila.

Jack himself did not have a wife. He never had, and seeing as he was now almost sixty-three years old, he thought it extremely unlikely that he would have one at any point in the future. This had been a source of regret for him at certain times in his life, but he chose not to dwell on it too often. That's that, he said to himself, whenever the regret reared its head. That's that.

Someone who didn't know Jack, who made judgements based on his appearance and his lifelong status as a bachelor, might get a few things wrong. They might look, for instance, at the ancient overalls he often wore, the tousled beard on his face. They might see the flaking paint outside and assume that the rooms in which he lived would be likewise unkempt, or even unclean. They might picture dirty dishes, and stacks of old newspapers against the walls. They might imagine him a hoarder, a man who filled every inch of space with things he would never need, and for whom the detritus of his life had become a kind of company.

But none of this was true. Jack's house was tidy. All of it. And the only thing he ever hoarded, other than solitude, was music. The front room of Hamar, which looked out on a field of Cheviot ewes, was packed with CDs and records, arranged in alphabetical order on the shelves. Jack's house was full to overflowing with songs.

If you looked at the first of these shelves, high up on the left beside the door, you would find Roy Acuff alongside Kay Adams. And if you looked at the last, over by the window, there would be Dwight Yoakam and Faron Young. For the music that Jack loved was country music. The songs he listened to, and sang, were country songs.

For a man in his sixties, Jack was fairly fit. He had a belly, naturally, and sometimes he looked at that mound of flesh and fat as though it belonged to someone else. It had appeared one day – that's how it seemed, at least – in his forties, and had never gone away. But it didn't slow him down. He walked every morning before breakfast, up the ridge behind the house to where the sea came into view. Just keeping myself acquainted, he would say, if anyone ever asked. But no one asked. If his neighbours had noticed these daily excursions, they didn't mention them to Jack.

There was an easy route up and over the hill, a little way north of the house. But that wasn't the route that Jack took.

Instead, he would stride the same steep path each time, his heartbeat climbing, the sweat prickling on his forehead. He wouldn't stop until he'd reached the highest point.

You could see a lot of water from up there. The land stumbled to an end at the bottom of the slope a few hundred yards beyond. You could see the broad sweep of St Magnus Bay, and scraps of land to the north and south. You could see the little beach where his father's boat had washed up the day after his parents drowned. Jack used to think about that sometimes when he was there. But these days he didn't think about much at all. He just scanned the horizon for a moment, turned around and went back home, his hunger rising with every step.

Breakfast was eggs, sometimes porridge. Toast, if he was feeling lazy. He'd eat it at the table, a place set for himself, with a cup of tea to wash it down. The hour depended on the season. In summer, he'd rise whenever he woke. It could be any time, really; the sun would be up. But in winter, it wasn't worth getting out of bed before nine. No point bumbling around in the darkness.

Most of his life, Jack's schedule had been more rigid. There had been more demands on his time. He'd worked as a postman for more than twenty years, picking up the mail in the morning in a rusting red Post Office van, then stopping at each house in turn to deliver. He'd liked it, mostly. He liked nodding and saying hello to his neighbours without needing to stop and speak. Got to crack on! he'd say, if anyone ever tried to talk to him for too long. He'd wave and away he'd go. But one morning, he'd had enough. He wanted to stay in bed and sleep. And though he didn't,

7

though he went to work as expected and did his round, he handed in his notice that afternoon, and that was that.

Afterwards, he'd done various jobs, often part-time. He drove a delivery van for a few years. Later, he'd been at Scatsta Airport, lugging bags on and off the helicopters and planes for the oil workers heading out to the rigs. And then Scatsta Airport closed down.

The thing was, having stayed on in the house that he'd inherited, having not had any children of his own, demands on Jack's wallet were never especially great. He needed to eat and to keep the electrics on and to fill the tank with heating oil when it ran low and to keep his car on the road. And he needed to buy music. But that was more or less it. He valued time more than money, and since the former was easier to accumulate than the latter, he'd done okay.

These days, Jack worked only an hour or two each evening during the week. He was called a janitor, but really he was a cleaner. He swept and hoovered the office of a salmon farm company in Treswick, three miles from his house. He emptied the bins, wiped the desks and scrubbed the bathroom floors. He replaced lightbulbs when they blew, but the work never got much more technical than that. He suspected the job had been given to him as a kind of favour.

There may have been those who thought of Jack as lazy – some, perhaps, had held that belief since he sold the croft, and nothing he'd done since then had disabused them – but anyone who'd asked for his help over the years had found him willing to lend a hand, without ever asking for a thing in return. People thought of him as a good man when they thought of him at all. And now that he was approaching the age of retirement, nobody resented the fact that he didn't work very hard.

After breakfast, his usual thing was to sit a while and read. Sometimes the news, on his computer. Sometimes a magazine. Sometimes a book. Whatever took his fancy. A few hours could pass like that, and they were often among the happiest hours in a day. There was a sense of luxury, for Jack, in putting his mornings to this use, in focusing himself on words. Eventually, though, that focus would soften and the desire for more tea would rise. He would get up from his armchair, or from the desk in the back bedroom where the computer lived. He would groan or sigh, often as not, in the way that those who live alone will allow themselves, and he would lumber, heavy-footed, to the kettle.

Jack was a big man. Not huge – he was six foot one, so just a few inches taller than average – but he was stocky and broad-shouldered, which made him seem larger, especially with that belly. Even the slight stoop he'd developed in the last few years – too much time hunched over his guitar, he thought, though his habit of walking with his head bowed was more likely to blame – even that had not diminished him. He would enter a room and people would look up. They would notice him. He had wished sometimes that he were smaller.

The second mug of tea of the day, Jack thought, was usually the best of all. It could provide a kind of reset, a new beginning. It would be somewhere between nine and twelve, most often, depending on the season and depending on his mood. The day was still young, in other words, and with that second small shot of caffeine inside him, he could survey the hours ahead and decide how best to spend them.

Sometimes, he would go back to his book, especially if the weather was poor. Or else he would put a CD in the stereo, and sit down to listen, his feet resting on a stool. But in summer, when it wasn't raining, Jack would often take his tea outside, stepping into his boilersuit and rubber boots by the door.

The garden, on the south side of the house, was a funny-shaped thing – twenty metres long, near enough, and six metres wide. When he'd sold the rest of the land, Jack had wanted to keep enough to grow a few vegetables, and he'd wanted the old shed as well. Between them, house and shed provided two sides of the garden. The other two sides – marked out, it seemed, in a moment of extreme disorientation – had a wire fence around, over which Jack crossed each morning as he set out for his walk.

It was more than he needed, and always had been. But he liked that. He liked to know that he could expand production if ever it seemed necessary. At least a third of the space was unused every year, and in the corner closest to the house he grew flowers instead of veg: a few spring bulbs, a perennial or two, and some pansies and sweet peas, like his mother used to grow. There were foxgloves as well, which sprung up in the most surprising of places, and those he liked very much indeed.

Just as Jack's home was spick and span, the garden, too, was tidy. He put in the time to make it so. He dug and hoed and watered and fed. He checked for caterpillars and for root fly and blight. As far as was possible, he kept everything in order. Now that his paid work was limited to the evenings, this was easier to do. The last few years, Jack's garden had been better than ever. Its flourishing sustained him, as much as he, with his devoted attention, sustained it.

After lunch (cheese on toast, on this occasion), Jack went to the shop. This was a regular excursion: two or three times a week he went, at least. Less often – twice a month, or so – he'd visit one or other of the supermarkets in Lerwick, fill the car with essentials and bring them home. But between-times, for his day-to-day needs, he'd drive a couple miles down the road to where a clutch of houses stood, with a well-stocked little shop among them.

He parked up and went inside. A bell jangled above the door. 'Hi aye,' he said, glancing behind the counter. Vina, the shop's owner, was there, a pair of spectacles perched like a tortoiseshell tiara on her silver-grey curls.

'Hi aye, Jackie,' she replied.

Vina had called him that, *Jackie*, for as long as he could remember. Her father had done the same, and she'd picked it up from him. Jack didn't like being Jackie, but he'd never told her so. After all, Vina wasn't Vina's name either, so he could hardly get too uppity about it. She was Violet, originally, but no one had called her that since she was at school.

Jack grabbed a basket and began to browse. He needed food for tonight and for the next night or two as well.

He opened one of the refrigerators in the furthest aisle, and pulled out a pack of mince. He checked the date on the label and set it in the basket.

'Mince and tatties for dinner, is it?' Vina called out from behind the counter.

There was no privacy in this place.

'I'm leanin that way,' he said.

'You had it last week as well,' Vina told him.

Jack sighed to himself. 'I reckon I'll survive,' he said.

He walked farther down the aisle, grabbed a bag of potatoes and a couple of carrots. At the back of the shop, he picked up a tin of tomatoes, then set it on the shelf again. Instead, he took some dried pasta and a jar of red sauce. Then a tin of baked beans, just in case.

'Did you hear aboot Ally Polson?' Vina asked, when Jack was halfway up the central aisle, lingering by the fancies.

Jack had not heard, and he said so.

'Stroke,' said Vina.

'Huh,' Jack said. He rejected a packet of date slices, and instead put a Jamaica ginger cake in the basket. 'Is he dead?'

'No,' said Vina. 'No quite.'

'Ach, well,' Jack nodded. 'Never mind.'

Vina made a noise that was half cackle and half gasp. 'Now now,' she said.

Of all the boys who had tormented Jack when he was young – and there were more than a few of them: bullies, and those who wished only to escape the attention of such people themselves – Ally Polson had been about the worst. As vicious with his words as with his fists. Jack saw him only rarely these days, and always from a distance; he had lived in Lerwick for many years. But from what Jack had heard, the man had not improved with age.

'I dunna think I'll miss him if he goes,' Jack added.

'You're no the first to say that,' Vina replied. Then she cleared her throat to indicate the subject was closed.

Vina had always been a talker, and a listener too. Always trading in other people's news. It was part of what qualified her to run a shop like this. Since Jack's own life was too uneventful to be of much interest to anyone else, he was rarely the subject of this news. But he liked to hear it. It was part of why he came in so often, rather than making more trips to town. The way the prices were in here he'd have been better off driving all those extra miles.

Vina was a year younger than Jack, and they had known each other all of their lives. Their fathers had been best friends, and Jack thought of her as his friend too – his best friend, really, though he wouldn't have put it like that. She was married to a man named Gordon whose health was bad. He used to work alongside Vina in the shop until he got so big and wheezy that he was pretty much immobile. When Covid first arrived in Shetland, a few years back, he stopped coming in at all. And after the lockdowns had passed, he never returned. Jack guessed that Gordon was housebound now, but he'd never asked. He didn't want to draw attention to the man's problems, and he didn't want Vina to think he was prying. She, in turn, was close to silent when it came to her own life. Over the years, she and Jack had probably spoken about every other person within an eight-mile radius of this spot, but never about her husband.

Jack took his basket to the counter, and set it beside the till. He looked around for a few seconds, certain he'd forgotten something, but he couldn't work out what it was. Vina picked the items up one by one to check the prices.

A packet of mince. A kilo of potatoes. Two carrots. Two tins of peaches. Dried pasta (the twisty ones). A jar of pasta sauce (red). A small loaf of sliced bread (brown). Half a dozen eggs. A tin of baked beans. A pot of cotton buds. A Jamaica ginger cake.

'Ears givin you trouble again?' Vina asked, as the cotton buds beeped beneath the scanner.

Jack didn't answer. He threw everything into the big jute bag he'd brought with him, then reached for his wallet to pay. He patted his chest, where it ought to have been. He was still wearing the boilersuit he'd put on to work in the garden earlier, and the wallet wasn't there. It was in his old corduroy jacket, hanging in the porch at home.

Vina shook her head and laughed. She pulled a black-and-red ledger book out from under the counter and wrote Jack's name inside. She printed a till receipt and clipped it to the page. 'We'll likely see you again in a day or twa, Jackie. You can settle up then.'

'Likely,' Jack said, and nodded in gratitude and apology.

'Enjoy your mince and tatties.'

He raised his hand to say goodbye, then jangled the door open and went outside.

Jack was drunk. Not foolish drunk. Not wearing-the-stetson-hat-that-hung-on-the-back-of-his-bedroom-door drunk. Just a mellow, warm-headed, three-tall-whiskeys drunk. Kentucky bourbon, to be precise. It was a comforting feeling, a syrupy glow, and it brought a certain kind of focus to his thoughts. Sometimes when he drank, he would sit with those thoughts, let them take shape and then undo themselves, let them keep him company. But mostly he would listen to music.

That night, it was the Louvin Brothers: lifelong favourites. He had known some of these songs since he was in his cradle, had known the words for longer than he had known what they meant. The music spilled from the speakers, and he closed his eyes to hear it better. Every so often, he would press the remote and skip back to the beginning of a song just to hear it again.

Jack was in his armchair, with his feet resting on the battered old kist that had long served as his coffee table. The kist, like the music, was older than he was, its wooden boards warped and discoloured. On his left side was the wall of CDs, from which he'd picked this one, and behind him were the records, which he didn't play so often these days. He liked the sound of them, liked the feel of them in his hands as well, but he couldn't be bothered to turn them over halfway.

The living room of Hamar felt smaller and more crowded now than it had done when Jack was growing up. The sheer quantity of music he'd amassed over the years – most of it bought from Clive's Record Shop in Lerwick, until it closed down – had seen to that. But still, this space was more familiar to him than anywhere else in the world. He had taken his first steps over there, beside the fire, and had almost fallen into the flames. He had slept in here many times as a boy, watched over by his great-grand-uncle Tom. He had so many memories of this room that it seemed not separate from him at all but a part of who he was and who he had always been. He had done so much of his living in this room.

Another song began. 'When I Stop Dreaming': the one that Jack loved most of all. He listened once, then played it again. It didn't matter how many times he heard it, the song always sounded bright and startling. It was something about the way the melody rose through the verse, untethered after the second line, towards that soaring final note. It was something about the way the brothers' voices coiled around each other in the chorus like the strands of a rope, tight and tense and impossible to pry apart. It was something about that strange last verse, the one about rocks that grow and rain that returns to the sky. It seemed to belong to a fable or a myth. It was a magical, beautiful yearning. It was a solid kick to the heart.

When he was younger, Jack had wished for a brother to sing with, to harmonise the way that Ira and Charlie Louvin had, the way the Delmore Brothers had, the way the Stanley Brothers had. He'd wanted to know what that would feel like, for his voice to be entwined with someone else's, to be bound in that mysterious, transcendent way to someone he loved. When his mother and father were alive, one or other of them would sometimes join in when they heard him mumbling a tune, but embarrassment, then, would cause him to stop. And so Jack had only ever sung alone, and for years – decades, now that he thought of it – he hadn't sung in anyone's company at all. Back in his twenties, when he drank a little more, he used to play at parties sometimes. Neighbours' houses, it would be, or friends from work. There were always parties. People eager to be entertained. There'd be fiddles, often, and Jack would sit in a corner and strum along as best he could. Then, at some point, late on, when the fiddlers took a break, attention might turn to him. Someone would request a song by Hank Williams, by Kris Kristofferson, by Willie Nelson. Play 'Blue Eyes Crying In The Rain', they'd say. Play 'Me And Bobby McGee'. Jack would do as he was told, but without much enthusiasm. He didn't want to be a jukebox. He'd sing the song then bow his head towards the strings, as if to fend off any more requests. On the few occasions he followed up with a song of his own, people just talked over him. Eventually, he stopped going altogether. He found the parties exhausting. It took so much effort just to be sociable. There'd be hardly anyone now, he guessed, who'd remember he could play at all.

Jack listened to the song one more time then switched the music off. He took another sip of bourbon and set the glass on the floor, then picked up the guitar that was leaning against the CDs beside him. It was a sunburst Martin acoustic that he'd bought after selling the croft. It was his most treasured possession by a very long way. He put a capo at the first fret, strummed a rich, sonorous chord, and tried to sing the song he'd just heard. It wasn't easy. It was too high for comfort, and the melody felt unnatural in his throat. Somehow the whole thing was lifeless with just one voice. He tried changing the key, but that didn't work either. The song faded away. He changed the chords, then he changed the words. They were nonsense at first, these new words, just vowels and consonants strung together in no particular order. He stretched one line and clipped another. He loosened the tune, twisted it out of shape, until it became unrecognisable, until it became something else entirely: a new song, not yet written. Jack followed it, tried to pin a corner of it down, a single solid line from which he could build outwards.

He found a structure for the verse – just four chords and a simple melody. Something that felt familiar. Something steady and reliable. Nothing that would knock him off balance. Had he been a little more sober he might have steered the tune in a more ambitious direction. But there was no real need for that now.

Jack found his line. He unearthed it, part from memory, part imagination. *My love lies over the wide ocean blue.* Sure, it wasn't quite grammatical, but there was something about it that Jack liked. The words seemed firm. Ancient, even. He wrote them in his notebook, and then sang them twelve, thirteen times in a row, to see where they might lead.

He knew then, from that single line, that this song would join the many others that had been written about loved ones who'd left, about restless sweethearts, about disappearing darlings. There must be thousands of such songs. Tens of thousands, maybe. And some of the best were country songs. Jack did not have a lover overseas, but he could imagine having one. He could picture himself jilted and abandoned. He could inhabit that role, certainly, for long enough to write a song.

This was something Jack did. It was something he had always done, since he first could strum a chord and hold a tune. Always, he had copied and learned other people's music, training his hands and his voice to replicate, as best he could, the songs he loved. But there was an energy left over, a hunger for songs that no one else had written. He would scribble them on scrap paper, and later, as now, in a notebook bought especially for the purpose. It was among the most pointless things that Jack did with his time, but it never felt like that in the moment. There was always an urgency that propelled him as he wrote, as though these words, this melody, needed to be written. He could never explain that, least of all to himself. But nor could he ignore it.

The bourbon was done, and Jack could feel it was hindering more than helping him now. He kept going, though, trying out lines in his head, singing them, writing them down, and then, when required, crossing them out again. By midnight, the song was more or less done. It was good enough for Jack. Good enough for now. Tomorrow morning, he might sit down in his back bedroom to record it. He would save the song in a folder on the computer. Then, most likely, he would never listen to it again.

# WIDE OCEAN BLUE

My love (she) lies over the wide ocean blue
In a ~~land~~ country that I've never seen
                                    old
She wanted to see this world for herself
                                    at home
So she sailed (off?) & left me alone

*✱ CHORUS*

                                        (might be)
I think of her often wherever she is
~~Broken~~
In love with that sweet foreign air
                                        so
I think of the arms that once held me close
                        midnight
(And) I think of her long ~~auburn~~ hair


✱ CHORUS

            long
Once in a while a postcard arrives
~~A few words of greeting is all~~
                                    still
~~She thinks~~ Her thoughts turn to home
                                it seems
I keep them all safe (beneath the bed) where I
So I'm over her in my dreams        sleep
   that

✱ CHORUS!
   I curse the distance between us
   I curse the wide ocean blue

                            (rpt.)

20

# the dreadful barrel

## 1958

The first time Sonny climbed to the lookout barrel of the *Southern Wayfarer*, he almost fell to the deck again, many metres below. His fingers were stiff and trembling as he gripped the rigging and hauled himself upwards, his limbs straining against him like disobedient animals. He was already shaking when he reached the steel ladder that would take him the last fifteen feet to the top. But instead of pushing on, Sonny lowered his head and looked down, saw the ship shrunken beneath him, the whole world swaying as though ready to topple. He felt himself turning inside out and closed his eyes just in time. He hung there, blind, until the sickness passed, and the strength returned to his arms.

Below, there was laughter. The Norwegian mate yelled to him, 'No eyes, no whales', then laughed again. Sonny pursed his lips and forced a breath between them. He reached one hand up to the ladder, and dragged himself the rest of the way. He landed in the crow's nest, and clung to its edge for the full hour of his watch, wishing every second of it that he were dead.

Now, months later, the fear had passed. The sickness, too. There was still a moment on every ascent when his stomach adjusted to the extra swing at that height, and to the sense of frailty that came with it. But he no longer paused on his way up. And he no longer looked down until he was safely at the top.

It was a changed world from up in the barrel: the ship, a trivial thing in the endless ocean. Sonny could see for miles in every direction. Miles of water and ice and sky, and of each melting into the other: a blue-white oneness. Sometimes, a vessel would be in view – another catcher, a buoy boat, or the floating factory – but often it was only them, waiting, watching, alone.

The hour would pass slowly, each minute stretched within Sonny's attention. He didn't dare let his eyes unfocus from the task, lest someone else should shout first from below. It was his job to see the whales, and he had the advantage of height. To miss one was to fail.

There were often seconds of uncertainty in that hour, of held breaths and a thudding heart. Far off, a tiny cumulus of spray: was it spindrift or spout? Time stopped as Sonny held his gaze, watching for confirmation: ocean or animal? A minute would pass, then another, and nothing. Or else a second cloud of mist would rise, more definite this time, and the certainty would grasp him as if by the throat. It would thrust him to the edge of the barrel, as it did now, and squeeze his lungs, as it did now, to shout: 'Hvalblast!' And again, 'Hvalblast!' He lifted his left arm to port, where the whales – two, five, more – had shown.

Everything after that happened fast. From the bridge, the call had already gone down for full speed, and the engines bellowed as the catcher accelerated: twelve, fourteen, sixteen knots. The ship lurched and galloped through the waves. Below him, all was action. The men had become a machine, each one of them in place, each one in some kind of motion. But Sonny saw none of it. His eyes were only on the water.

As the distance between them narrowed, he could see they were blues, with tall, silver spouts like pillars of mist. A mother and calf, and six more adults besides. This was what the men had been waiting for: the big whales that would bring them their bonuses. There had been too few this year. Too many empty horizons. Everybody knew what that meant. It was just a matter of time. The whispers, each season, grew louder: this one would be the last.

An hour passed and they were getting close. Sonny heard shouting from below, and saw the gunner ready himself at the bow, his whoops and wild gestures taking them the last hundred and fifty yards.

Hundred and thirty.

Hundred and ten.

Hundred.

Closer.

The gunner was watching the biggest of the whales, his whole body pointed towards the animal. Sonny, from high above, could almost feel the man's finger tighten around the trigger.

Closer.

The whale dived.

Sonny didn't breathe. His heart paused. He was eyes alone.

Looking.

Looking.

Looking.

There!

Fifty feet away, a string of bubbles as the whale approached the surface. 'Comin up! Comin up!' Sonny yelled, and the gunner leaned forward, the barrel of the harpoon gun pointed at the spot where the great dark shape emerged to meet the air, emerged to meet the awful sound that ricocheted through everything, through its ocean and through its body, its enormous punctured body.

The harpoon detonated. Sonny took a breath.

Below, everything continued. The line hurtled out as the whale dived again, its efforts to escape this fate as audacious as they were futile. The ship slowed to let the creature run, and when it showed again, another blast. The water churned scarlet and the monstrous animal stilled.

They moved swiftly then: a wire wrapped around the tail, a tube thrust inside to inflate the beast's belly and keep it from sinking. A flag was impaled in the flesh, a transmitter too, so the buoy boat could find the body and tow it to the factory.

Sonny kept his eyes on the other whales. He watched as they fled, growing smaller, until the engine growled back into pursuit. There was no stopping the catcher now.

In the coming hours, they killed six, one after the other. Only the mother and calf were spared. A joke, really. An awful joke. All this slaughter, and still the pretence of mercy. Still the pretence of preservation.

For the men, for Sonny, it was a day of triumph and relief.

# 2

Besides the blue wooden house at the other end of the track – which was called Puffin Cottage, though Jack refused to speak that mawkish name aloud – there were few buildings in the immediate vicinity of Hamar. There was an old croft house, long abandoned now, on the opposite side of the main road from the blue house, but the nearest inhabited one was half a mile away. That belonged to Old Andrew, who was still living, just about. Beyond that stood a sparse huddle of houses, built when Jack was a teenager, and two modern ones, wooden, constructed at the same time and in the same ostentatious style as that of his nearest neighbours.

He knew the names, occupations, and in many cases the extended family connections of all those who lived in these houses. And the same was true for another few miles down that road, as far as the shop and a little way beyond. He wasn't quite so sure about the other direction. There were places that had sold recently to people from elsewhere, and

Jack hadn't learned yet who they were. His principal source of information was Vina at the shop. The limits of her knowledge were the limits of his.

Jack didn't think of himself as a gossip – he had few occasions to share what he learned from Vina with anyone else; he was a consumer of it rather than a dealer – but nor did he consider his interest to be merely nosiness. It was part of knowing his place, that was all, like knowing the names of streets or shops or train stations. It was the human topography of his particular corner of the world, and understanding it, Jack thought, was essential to his feeling at home.

Other than Valsetter, where the shop was located – barely even a hamlet, let alone a village – the nearest settlement of any size was Treswick, three miles of winding road in the opposite direction. There was a shop there too – it really *was* a village – but Jack had no loyalty to the current owner of that one, and so he rarely went inside. Treswick was where he'd gone to primary school, and where his postal round had started each day, when the Post Office was still there. Now, almost the only reason he drove in that direction was for work, five evenings a week. The company he cleaned for had its office and storeroom there, down by the harbour. Dusky red and rectangular, it was the largest building in Treswick by some distance.

Jack pushed the hoover beneath the desk, making sure he covered both corners with the brush. Forward, back, forward, back. The chair beside him almost toppled in the process, and he pulled the nozzle from the machine and scraped it over the seat. He turned towards the next desk, his feet stepping in time with the music in his ears. The headphones didn't quite block the drone of the vacuum cleaner, but when he turned them up loud the machine was barely audible. The music filled his head and moved his body.

You wouldn't call it dancing, exactly, what Jack was doing. Even without the hoover in his hand it wouldn't have looked like that. But if someone had arrived and observed him like this – as once had happened, in fact, when Janice, the company secretary, came in late to collect something and stumbled upon this very sight, then slipped away again before Jack had noticed she was there – they'd have seen a man in thrall to rhythm.

He had a playlist that he'd compiled especially for the hours he spent cleaning. It was long enough to last him a week at work without repetition. The criteria for inclusion were not strict. The songs didn't need to be too pacy; he would follow the beat where that was possible, or else he would move at half-speed with the faster ones. The only rule he'd stuck to as he curated the list was that songs in waltz time were unconducive to vacuuming, and were therefore disallowed.

Right now he was listening to Johnny Rodriguez, 'Ridin' My Thumb To Mexico'. He'd never have included this one on a list of his favourite tracks – even a long list – but it was good for this purpose. There was the right kind of swing to it, and a meld of Spanish guitar and Texas twang that Jack enjoyed. It was also short. It sprang into life, and then it was gone.

He switched the vacuum cleaner off and unplugged it, pressed his foot on the button to retrieve the lead, then wheeled the machine into the cupboard at the top of the stairs. In his ears, Connie Smith began to belt out 'Just For What I Am'. He went back into the open-plan office, took the yellow cloth and canister of spray and began wiping down the five desks. Most had pens, folders and sheets of paper strewn on either side of the computers, and these he lifted, wiped beneath, then replaced. He knew better than to tidy anything away. Jack's job was to go unnoticed.

Once the office was done, it was just the kitchenette next door and the bathroom at the bottom of the staircase left to go. They wouldn't take him long. A few squirts of disinfectant and an extra toilet roll, then a splash round with the mop. Sometimes there were dishes to clean, but mostly the staff did those for themselves, and once a week he would sweep the big storeroom at the other side of the building, but that was tomorrow's task. For now, he was done.

It was a few weeks after he first took on this job when Jack realised that he liked it. That was a surprise. When Douglas Inkster, who ran the company – Shetland Salmon Services & Supplies, a name whose absurd initials adorned the row of vehicles outside – called him up one Friday afternoon, Jack had not been enthusiastic. He agreed that he did need some work, yes, he just wasn't sure if this was right for him. In hindsight, his reticence was merely pride. Not that he felt himself above it; he was willing to do anything that didn't ask too much of him. But he detected pity in the offer, and that he didn't like. Douglas could easily have found a proper cleaner and paid them close to minimum wage. Instead, he described it as 'a janitorial position', and suggested a generous weekly rate. There had always been those who had treated Jack as something of a charity case – orphan Jack, solitary Jack, an unfortunate man all round. Even now, in his sixties, he was still conscious of that commiserative gaze upon him. Jack did not like to be pitied, but nor could he afford to turn down a wage, and so, the following Monday at five o'clock, he let Douglas walk him through what needed doing, and then he did it.

What Jack liked about the job, he realised, other than the fact it was untaxing and could be done at whatever pace and time suited him, was that, when he walked out of the door each evening, the place looked better than it had when he'd walked in. Not dramatically better – he came too often for it to ever look especially unclean – but it looked fresher, tidier, well cared for. And aside from the first week, when he'd made the mistake of moving thing into neat piles on people's desks, then received a phone call urging him to stop, Douglas and his colleagues seemed happy with his work. They smiled and chatted whenever he bumped into them. They left him a card and a bottle of wine at Christmas to say thank you. Douglas had even paid him in full during those months of the pandemic when he'd hardly come in to work at all. Of the handful of jobs he'd held in his life, this one might have been his favourite. He would happily continue for as long as he was able.

Jack closed the glass front door behind him, rubbed a smudge away with his sleeve, then locked it. He checked the handle, just in case, and dropped the key in his coat pocket. In the mid-evening light, a curlew burbled over the field across the road, the song cranking up like an old motor, then lilting back again towards silence as the bird descended. Jack listened, then opened the door of his car and sat down. He'd eaten dinner before he came out, but now he was hungry again. The ginger cake would be waiting for him when he got home.

By the time he turned onto the road that led up to the house, Jack's stomach was rumbling. Maybe he'd need more than a slice of cake after all. In his mind, he opened the fridge and the kitchen cupboards to see what the options were. Cheese and oatcakes, maybe. A tin of soup. A second slice of cake. Nothing jumped out as satisfying this particular hunger.

He pulled up at the end of the track and switched off the engine. The lambs on the other side of the fence were making a racket, skipping back and forth across the field as though no greater game could be imagined. Once in a while, a mother would look up from her munching to check that no harm was being done. Then she'd look down again at the grass.

Jack closed the car door and headed for the house, on the uneven flagstone path that his father had laid more than fifty years before. Despite repeated attempts at repair over the decades, some of those stones still refused to lie flat. They wobbled at even the lightest of steps. Jack long ago learned which ones to tread upon and which to stride over. As he walked, he was still thinking about his empty belly and ways to fill it, which was why he failed to notice the cardboard box on the doorstep until he was almost on top of it.

It was an ordinary brown box, square, and the top was

folded closed without tape. There was no name or address written on it, so it must have been delivered by hand. He couldn't imagine what it might be.

Jack leaned down. He put his hands out, braced, but when he took hold of the box and lifted, it weighed hardly anything at all. And whatever it was in there was not stable. He felt the weight shift from one side to the other, as if it were tipping, though he held his arms straight out in front of him. He pushed the door open and set the box on the table in the porch.

Then he heard it: a scratch against the cardboard from inside, and a high-pitched mew. The tucked flaps on top rose up, and another sharp cry emerged.

'What in the hell?' Jack said, then nudged the door shut with his foot.

He put two fingers beneath one of the flaps and pulled, gently, peering into the space between, but it was too dark inside to see anything. He pulled harder, and the top sprung open, and in that same instant in which the contents of the box were revealed, the living part of those contents – a black kitten, with a single white paw – exited at high speed, raced around the porch for several seconds in search of an escape route, and then cowered beneath the table. The only thing left inside the box was a small towel on which the animal had been sitting.

'What in the hell?' Jack said again. It was the only sentence he'd spoken all day, and now he'd said it twice.

He stood back and looked at the kitten, which held him with a gaze that was two parts fear, one part defiance. It was waiting to see what he would do next.

Jack had absolutely no idea what he would do next. He was still trying to catch up with what had already happened. And so the pair of them looked at each other in silence for a long time. In the end, it was the cat that acted first. It gave another of its little mews: a kind of question, it seemed like, and the only question right now for which Jack had an answer.

'No,' he said, 'I'll no hurt you.'

The kitten's stance softened at the tone of his voice. It lowered its back end to the tiles, but its eyes didn't stray from him, even for a second.

Jack was trying to muster some certainty now, and the only thing he could hold on to was the fact that, wherever this little creature had come from, it would need to go back. He assumed that someone was playing a practical joke on him. He would just need to work out who that was and the solution would be simple. He would return it to whomever the joker had been, and laugh along with them for a moment then come home again. Ha ha ha, he'd say. Yes, well done. You got me.

Jack shook his head. It wasn't the first time he'd been the target of local pranksters. Not by a long shot. On the last occasion, a couple of years back, he'd seen something flapping around through the back windscreen of his car as he was driving. When he stopped to check it out, he found a pig's tail tied to his wipers. He guessed it was the Simpson boys from the big farm that had done it, but he never bothered to find out. He just dumped the thing on the ground and drove on.

Before that, twice in the space of a month, he found one tyre of his car resting inside a plastic fish box: as good as a wheel-clamp, near enough. It must have taken a group of them to organise that, walking up the track in the darkness, lifting the back of the car and sliding the box beneath, then running off into the night laughing. He'd had to phone round several of the men from nearby to give him a hand getting it out. And though he didn't so much as mention his suspicions, they might well have been the same men who'd put it in there in the first place. It was funny, Jack thought, how pity and mockery could be kin.

The kitten seemed restless now, and Jack wondered if it might need the toilet. He considered opening the front door and letting it run, to find its own way back to wherever it came from. But he decided against it. It felt like the wrong solution. The kitten was as much the victim of this prank as Jack was, and since it was no more than a few months old by the looks of it, it probably wouldn't survive very long on its own.

As he knelt down in front of the kitten to see what kind of scared it was – would it approach him if he put out his hand, he wondered – a more benign story occurred to him. He remembered a few months back, at the shop, when he'd bumped into Sarah, the woman from next door (he always used that term, 'next door', though the two houses were at least two hundred yards apart). She'd been chatty that day, as she usually was, and had mentioned something about Vaila, her daughter, wanting a pet. It was something about responsibility, about her not being old enough, and the argument they'd had on the subject. Jack had nodded along at the time, but he hadn't retained the details.

Maybe that was it. Maybe Sarah had changed her mind,

and someone had delivered a cat to the wrong house. Or else maybe she'd got the impression in their conversation that *he* wanted a kitten. That didn't seem likely, when he thought about it, but he could sometimes get a little flustered when he spoke, and so it wasn't impossible that he'd said something stupid.

He would go and speak to her, he decided. It was the only way to be sure.

'Will you be all right?' Jack asked the cat, having decided it was best not to take it with him. The cat lifted its head a little, and he noticed for the first time a patch of white beneath its chin, a tiny bib to match its one white paw. It looked like it would be okay.

He took the car. It was lazy of him, sure, but the situation needed to be resolved. And anyway, he was still hungry. The sooner he got this sorted, the sooner he could eat.

He stopped in the middle of the track and turned off the engine. He left his door wide open and went up the path to the big blue house. The garden out front was sparse and untidy: a wild rose bush in one corner, and a scabby patch of lawn. He stepped onto the raised porch and rapped at the door, and as he did so he felt the certain knowledge that he was about to make a fool of himself. The kitten was not Sarah's. Of course it wasn't. It had nothing to do with her. This was a ridiculous errand, and he should have realised that before setting out.

Jack rubbed his hand over his face, scratched his beard, trying to concoct another purpose for his trip in order not to sound like a buffoon. He came up blank. The door opened, and Sarah smiled.

'Jack,' she said, bright as could be. 'Lovely to see you. Is everything okay?'

She was nearly always like this, Sarah: cheerful and, as far as Jack could tell, pleased to see him. She looked tired this evening, her eyes heavy, but that was hardly surprising. She worked all week in a care centre, and she looked after her daughter alone. That she was still awake at all seemed miraculous to Jack. He liked Sarah. Had such things as friendship come more naturally, he would have liked for them to be friends. He would have liked to speak to her as easily as she would sometimes speak to him. As it was, he considered her a good neighbour, a person he could trust. In some uncertain way, he had expected Sarah to move on after her husband walked out, to find somewhere smaller, more manageable for just the two of them. And he was glad, when he thought of it, that she had not.

Jack looked at his feet, then up again, before he spoke. 'Well, no exactly, no. I was just . . .' He sighed. 'I was just wonderin if you'd seen onybody come up the road in the past hour or twa?'

'Up your road?'

'Yeah.'

Sarah twisted her mouth to show that she was thinking. 'Well,' she said, 'I heard a car going up ten minutes ago. Is that what you mean?'

'No. That was me.'

'Ah, okay. Well, I think I *might* have heard someone an hour or so back. But that could have been on the main road. I'm not sure. I wasn't looking out the window at the time. Why? Has something happened?'

Jack sighed again, as though exhausted. 'Ach, it's just, well, I think someen's playin a joke on me, that's all. And I'm tryin to figure oot wha it is.'

'What kind of joke?' Sarah cocked her head to one side.

'They've left a cat at the hoose,' Jack said. 'In a box.'

Sarah looked at him for a few seconds, as if interpreting his words, then burst out laughing. She covered her mouth with one hand, and Jack saw that she still wore her wedding ring.

'Sorry,' she said. 'Sorry! I don't mean to laugh. That just wasn't what I expected you to say.'

'What were you expectin me to say?' Jack asked.

'Nothing in particular. Nothing. Just not that.'

'No, well, I didna expect it either. But now there's a cat in the porch and I havna a clue what I'm meant to do wi it.'

Sarah was only just keeping her face straight. 'You could drive around and knock on every door until somebody confesses, I suppose.'

'That doesna seem very practical,' Jack said.

'No, it wouldn't be. And I wasn't being serious.'

'Ah, okay.' Jack was sometimes so intent on seeming sensible that he could miss a joke entirely.

'Maybe you just need to keep it in the house for now. Surely whoever left it will come and pick it up later.'

Jack shrugged his shoulders. 'I hope so,' he said. But he didn't feel much hope.

'We had a cat when I was little,' said Sarah, adjusting her position against the doorframe, and looking down at her feet. 'It was the funniest thing. He used to sing whenever we watched the television. Or not *sing* exactly, but, you know, the tomcat equivalent. It used to drive my mother berserk. She'd grab him by the scruff of the neck and throw him out of the house when he made that noise. She couldn't stand it.'

'Huh,' said Jack. He wasn't yet sure how this story was connected to his predicament, or if indeed it was at all. But he was listening.

'I loved him, though,' she went on. 'Adored him. He used to sleep on my bed every night, and wake me up at four a.m., like clockwork. I didn't mind, though. He could do no wrong in my eyes.' She was smiling at the memory as it came back to her, still looking down at the slippers on her feet.

'And what happened to him?' Jack asked, because he had to ask something.

'He got old and fat, got diabetes, then died,' Sarah said. 'For the last couple of years he was a sorry-looking creature, dragging himself around, half-blind. I'd left home by that stage, and I think my parents were just keeping him alive because they missed me or something. Poor thing!' She shook her head, then looked up at Jack again. 'Well, I'm sorry for rambling on like that,' she said. 'And I'm sorry I couldn't be more helpful.'

'Dunna worry. I'm sorry for botherin you. I just didna ken wha else to ask.'

'I'm glad you did,' Sarah said. 'I imagine it must be a bit of a puzzle. But you've given me something to laugh about this evening, and I'm grateful for that. So thank you.'

Jack nodded. Sarah's words had seemed, even to his

untrained ears, like an invitation to ask something more. But he wasn't certain of it. And he didn't know what that more might be. 'You're welcome,' he told her, which wasn't the right response at all. He turned around, away from the house. 'I'd better be off,' he said, already leaving, his hand raised. 'I'll need to see to this creature.'

'I hope you figure it out,' Sarah said to his back. He thought he heard her laugh again, but he didn't look round.

The kitten was still where he'd left it, beneath the table, and it cowered visibly as he opened the door into the porch. 'Now, then,' he said, keeping his voice low, so as not to frighten it more. 'I'm guessin you're hungry too.' He took his jacket off and hung it on a peg. 'Just stay here a moment, and I'll sort somethin oot for you.'

He opened the inside door, as narrowly as he could in case the cat tried to run inside. But it stayed where it was, just watching. 'Ach,' Jack said aloud, and pulled the door closed again. He went to the kitchen and rummaged in the corner cupboard. He found an old tin of tuna, and took two small bowls off the shelf. He emptied the fish into one of them and half-filled the other with water.

'Christ!' he said to himself. 'What a bloody thing.'

# DEAR NO ONE

I was on the shore this morning
Throwing stones and wasting time
I found a message in a bottle
That once ~~hot~~ Down on the waterline
~~And I broke~~ that bottle open
couldn't get
So I broke the glass instead
I picked the ~~papers~~ letters off the grand and this is what it said:

Dear No one, pleased to meet you I'm
thinking of you, my old friend (x2)

Nothing else was written, ~~didn't~~
could
I didn't know what I ~~might~~ mean
So I ~~put it in my pocket~~
Folded up that paper in the pocket of my jeans
Then I went about my business, using up
my precious time
But I couldn't seem to get that message off my mind

CHORUS

nearly?
It was almost one week later
I was drinking up some wine
When I emptied out my bottle I knew that it
was time
So I took that letter out again
And sealed it up inside   me/be
I took it to the shore and
Sent/gave that letter to the tide  sea

CHORUS

# the return

## 1958

When the *Southern Wayfarer* returned to the island of South Georgia at the end of the whaling season, it was late March. The men had not set foot on soil or stone in more than four months. They had been in constant motion. Steaming, lurching, swaying. Sonny felt landsick, his legs braced against the ground as though it couldn't be trusted. He stood on the shore at Leith Harbour, put his hands on his knees and leaned over to steady himself. Everything – the noise, the smell, the rusting chaos of the place – felt too much to bear.

At the edge of that rickety village, Sonny sat on a boulder, the cold rock jutting into his buttocks. He breathed a long, deep breath, and for the first time in months he felt the great relief of aloneness. The luxury of it. He was far enough from the harbour then that the sound of human voices had blurred into a murmur, no more decipherable than the babble and honk of the penguins just around the bay. He closed his eyes, listened to the hum of the wind in the mountains above; the hum of engines and machinery; the hum that lived inside his head after all those weeks at sea.

On his previous trip, Sonny had spent a winter in South Georgia (a winter that, back home, had been summer – a fact he had never quite got used to). Two seasons on the factory ship, working as a mess boy, with another season on the island in between. More than a year and a half in total, thousands of miles from home. He'd done it to prove that he could, to his friends, to his parents, to himself. And he'd done it for the money, too. That's what all of them were after, in the end. Or almost all. A few of the men were escaping things elsewhere, and a few just couldn't cope with a landlocked life. But for most, it was necessity that brought them south. The whaling was hard, ugly work, but back home there was next to nothing. Shetland offered few opportunities. It offered poverty, drudgery. Sonny's father had urged him to go, to take this job with Salvesen. In return, his family gained a little space in the house.

When the men got home, they would feel rich. Some would waste their money, fritter it on drink, on fancy motorbikes, on things they didn't need. But Sonny wasn't like that. When he went home, he worked. He would help out on his uncle's herring boat, or else just pick away at whatever bits of employment he could find. The money, he saved. He knew it would be needed.

During the season, whether on the floating factory or the catcher, Sonny did okay. Even working in the mess, as he'd done those first two years – helping the cooks in the galley, cleaning tables and serving food – he did okay. He was always busy and on the move, there was always something on which to focus his thoughts. But here in South Georgia, he was not okay. Here, he was stuck, and so very far from home. It caught him sometimes, that feeling, like a thump in the guts. Everything that mattered was elsewhere. The winter he spent on the island had been the worst time of his life. Boredom had become despair. There had been days when, hopeless and homesick, he had felt a noise building inside him, a roar, a scream, deep in his body, that would have rattled every glass pane and corrugated roof in this place if he had ever let it out. It was a visceral, physical disgust. It was anger: at himself and at the world, at the distance between one place and another, between one moment and the next. It was a nameless, shapeless horror.

Often, during that terrible winter, Sonny had thought about Ernest Shackleton, whose crossing of South Georgia's mountains forty years before was part of the mythology of this place, part of the story its visitors told themselves, as if they too could be touched by his courage and heroism. He was here, still, Shackleton, his body buried twelve miles down the coast, in the shadow of a tall granite headstone. What a fate that was, Sonny thought, to be left here on this island. He would rather go unburied than lie for ever in this godforsaken ground.

This year, they were just a week in Leith Harbour before sailing north again. A week in which Sonny never felt well. He walked among the white and grey timber buildings, the clutter of mud and rusting metal around his feet, the stink of whale in his throat. He did what work was asked of him, grateful for the distraction. In the evenings, he played cards or dominos to pass the time. He waited.

The day before they left South Georgia, six of the men were tasked with rounding up penguins. Edinburgh Zoo wanted a dozen gentoos, and they took fifteen, just to be sure. The birds in the colony were incautious things, half-tame, so gathering them was easy. Even those that sensed danger at the last minute couldn't waddle fast enough to escape. The men grasped the penguins tightly around the wings, then lifted them like unruly toddlers in their arms.

Sonny volunteered to look after the birds in their enclosure on the deck of the *Southern Venturer*. It was his job to keep them fed, and, as the weather warmed on the journey north, to keep them cool as well, spraying them with salt water, protecting them from the sun. The penguins were fine company, chattering to each other in a good-natured way, looking at Sonny with what seemed like curiosity. He would stand with them, watching as they ate, and for a time he would feel grateful for their presence and guilty for their imprisonment at once. He found himself fond of them, looking forward to his time on deck each day. Secretly, he gave them names. He learned to distinguish one from the other: variations in that band of white across the head, a damaged wing on one, a darker beak on another. He fancied some more self-assured, and others shy.

A week or so into the journey, a storm in the Forties tossed the *Southern Venturer* as if it were nothing. Waves swallowed them, then spat them out, knocking the enormous ship one way then another, lifting the bow, then slamming it down again. Water surged up the back of the vessel, flooding the deck, and two of the penguins were washed out of their enclosure, down the chute and into the furious ocean. When he saw they were gone, Sonny felt a muddle of emotions (so often feelings came to him like that: in a knot he was ill-equipped to undo). He felt something like grief at the loss of the birds, and, as well, something like pride or relief at their escape. He told himself they might find their way home, but he couldn't quite believe it was true.

Around half of the six hundred men on board the ship were Norwegian. The others were mostly Scots, and among them nearly a hundred Shetlanders. The two nationalities worked alongside each other every day, but at night, most often, they would socialise apart. The men seemed drawn, more and more as the voyage went on, to voices like their own. The Highlanders spoke Gaelic to one another, the Shetlanders talked among themselves, the few Glaswegians huddled. They were regrouping, it seemed to Sonny, becoming themselves again as their time at sea approached an end. When they did get together in the evenings, drunk, as many of them would be, it was usually for music.

There were nine fiddles on board that year, and at least two dozen men who could play, most of them from Shetland. There were accordions, too, and a concertina. Some of the Norwegians had guitars, and would sing, now and again. Sonny could follow along well enough – he had learned the basics of the language during his winter in Leith Harbour – but it always felt like an effort. The Scots had songs of their own, too, but they didn't accompany them with instruments.

One warm evening, near the equator, in a cabin just down the corridor from Sonny's, the fiddles were in full flight.

They were led by Davie Williamson, from Unst. There were four of them playing, and they all knew the tunes, but it was Davie who was pushing them, playing faster as the others struggled to keep up. A Norwegian fellow with a thick blonde beard was holding a guitar, strumming every now and then, but he couldn't keep pace. More than a dozen men were packed into the little room, clapping hands and stamping their feet in time. Sonny was one of them.

There were cheers when the tune finished, and there were handshakes for Davie, who always enjoyed attention. The noise of the cabin rose to fill the space the music had left behind. The voices and the laughter grew louder. And then, in amongst it all, a chord was played, and another one just behind it.

The Norwegian began to sing.

The first couple of lines were lost amid the din, but the crowd quietened as the song went on. The words clarified. Sonny knew this one. He'd heard it often enough, on record, at friends' and neighbours' houses. But he'd never really paid attention until now. Sonny wasn't much interested in music, truth be told. It rarely stepped beyond the background of his attention. He listened to the wireless for the news and weather, that was all. There were singers he liked well enough: Tony Bennett and Frank Sinatra, say. Men with real voices, rich and sweet. But he wouldn't go out of his way to listen.

This fellow, the Norskie, was no Sinatra. His voice was thin and nasal, his pronunciation eccentric. It wasn't clear he understood all the words that he was using. A few of the men smirked at each other across the cabin. But there was something about the song, there and then, that held Sonny's focus, some intensity to it that he'd never felt before. It was in the movement of the notes, the twang and bounce of them. And it was in the words, too. Again and again, slow and insistent, it returned to that dark, tormented line: 'I'm so lonesome I could cry'.

Sonny listened, and as he did so he found himself thinking of home. He found himself thinking of his parents and his siblings – his two older brothers and his little sister, Mary. He was thinking of Walter, too, the boy he'd signed up with, the first year he went to the whaling. They'd ended up on different ships when the season began, so Sonny didn't know until weeks later that Walter was dead. He had stepped off the side one morning; the first mate saw him go, but they never found him. It wasn't unusual. Some folk just couldn't take it, and the only escape was overboard. Sonny had tried not to think too much about Walter in the two years since, but here he was again. Vivid as he ever had been.

Davie the fiddler had joined in now, his bow drawing the melody out between the verses. He wasn't showing off this time, he was letting his music shine on someone else. The Norwegian, having run out of words, returned to the beginning, and played it through again. Sonny's thoughts seemed shaped by what he was hearing. The song arrived inside him as if it had lived there all along, as if he had known it for ever. It sounded brand new and as ancient as the world. Though he knew Hank Williams's name, he had no idea then that he was more than five years dead.

When the song finished, the applause, though not as raucous as it had been for the fiddles, was nonetheless whole-hearted. Someone shouted for more, and the Norwegian, pleased with himself, began to strum again. This time, he sang 'Hey Good Lookin'', aiming exaggerated winks at Geordie, one of the cooks, who was standing against the far wall. Everyone roared with laughter at that, and the strange spell of the last song was lifted.

In his cabin that night, staring up at the bunk above him, Sonny resolved to spend a little of the cash he had earned on a record player of his own. The way the song had made him feel that night – the strange force of it – he wanted to take that feeling home.

# 3

Vina's shop opened most days at 8.30 a.m. That morning, Jack arrived at twelve minutes past the hour, and he was in no mood to wait. He made himself visible, standing at the window beside the door. Green paint was flaking from the wood frame, and he picked at it with his thumbnail. He knew Vina would be inside, pottering about, getting things ready for the day, and it was just a matter of time before she looked up – and yes, there she was, by the storeroom entrance, hand on her chest, staring at him.

She came to the door and unlocked it.

'Bloody hell, Jackie! You coulda geen me a heart attack. I thought you were the grim reaper, come to carry me awa.' She shook her head as he stepped past her into the shop. 'So, what is it, then?' she asked. 'What's brought you in at this time of the mornin? Milk? Coffee? Bog roll?'

Jack glared. 'Cat food,' he said.

Vina cleared her throat. 'I'm guessin there's a story to

be telt,' she replied, then pointed. 'It's in the far corner, past the freezers.'

Jack was already en route. He knew as well as she did where everything in the shop was located. He grabbed what he needed: one yellow box of dry cat food, turkey flavour, that rattled as he picked it up, and a little sack of litter.

When he'd woken that morning, the kitten was mewing so loudly he could hear it from his bed. He went to the porch and opened the door a crack, and the stench almost felled him. The thing had pissed and shat in the corner furthest from where he'd laid its towel, and there was a look on its face that seemed to say, *I know, I know, but what did you expect me to do?* Then it ran, galloped, between Jack's legs and into the house. It took him ten minutes to find it again, cowering beneath the armchair in the spare room. It looked so miserable in there that he couldn't bring himself to drag it out. He left the house without taking his walk, without even eating breakfast.

'Well,' said Vina, as Jack put the food and litter on the counter and fumbled for his wallet. 'The least you owe me is an explanation. Last I kent, there was no cat resident at Hamar.'

Jack huffed. 'There's still no cat resident,' he said. 'Not permanently, onyway.' And then he told her the story.

Vina laughed more than seemed necessary to Jack. At one point, she was bent over, hooting, with her hands on her knees.

'It doesna seem that funny to me,' he said.

'That's what *makes* it so funny,' Vina told him, which he didn't understand at all.

'So what'll you do wi it?' she asked, once her laughter had subsided.

Jack shook his head. 'If someen doesna show up and claim it today, I'll take it to the shelter, I suppose. Or just droon it. Save myself some time.'

'Yeah, that'll be right,' Vina said, raising an eyebrow. 'There's plenty of folk would kill a kitten, right enough, but I dunna think you're wan of them.'

Jack didn't argue. She wasn't wrong.

'Will you keep an ear oot?' he said. 'Someen'll likely be in wantin to share the joke, so you can let me ken wha it is.'

Vina put two fingers to her temple and gave a salute. 'Absolutely,' she said. 'I'll call you if I hear.'

Jack nodded. He was not convinced that she would do that. She seemed too pleased with the thought of his situation to want to put an end to it. 'I need to get back,' he said.

'You certainly do. Go and feed your friend.' She grinned.

Jack made an indeterminate noise, half grunt, half grumble. He almost left the shop without taking his things, then turned back, picked them off the counter and went to the door.

In the short time he'd been away from the house, the kitten's mood had improved. Perhaps the change of scenery had eased its fear, or perhaps it was just too young to sustain anxiety for long. Either way, when Jack returned, striding into the living room in his socked feet, the cat was there, perched sphinx-like on the old floral sofa. It looked at him for some kind of sign: would it need to run and hide again, or could it just stay put? Jack looked away, not wishing to frighten it by staring. Better to know where it was, to gain its trust, so he could get it back in the box again when required. He'd been planning to go to town tomorrow anyway, so he could stop at the cat shelter en route to drop it off.

He found an old paint tray and filled it with litter, then showed it to the kitten, in the hope it would understand. He set it on the brown patterned lino of the kitchen floor. He put some food and water at the other side of the room, shaking the box to let the cat know what was happening.

Though Jack was hungry too, the change in his morning routine had unsettled him, and so he went to the porch again, pulled his boots back on, and set off up the hill for his walk. Twice now this creature had left him famished. The view from up on the ridge would surely bring him back to himself.

It was, then, that long season of anticipation in the garden, when all of the vegetables were growing, spreading, flourishing, but none yet were ready to be eaten. If he'd planted salad – lettuce, rocket, that kind of thing – Jack might have a few leaves to harvest by now. But he'd never been much of a salad eater, and the plants tended to flower and grow bitter before he ever made a dent in the crop. Sometimes he sowed them regardless, but this year he hadn't bothered.

Jack was looking at the vegetable patch, from the bench behind the house, but he wasn't thinking about it. His thoughts were drifting, and he was chasing a tune in his head. It wasn't anything in particular, the tune – or if it was, he couldn't name it – but the notes arose like stepping stones in front of him, one then another, and he knew, almost without question, where he needed to go.

Jack had often thought how peculiar music was in that way, how unlike language, in which a word could open up the possibility of a hundred others. In music, there were patterns and predictable routes, so that even in a song you'd never heard before, you would get a sense, quickly, of where it was going. There could still be surprises, of course, and leaps of logic. But Jack could hold a note in his mind and know there were only a small number of ways to move on from it, just a handful of possible paths to follow.

It made music seem deficient, to think of it that way, like a book composed of only a dozen words. But once you factored in all the other variables across the span of a song, it wasn't like that at all. A song was like a journey, or a story, with a starting point and a destination; no matter how similar the route, the details would always be different.

Or else, maybe, a song was like an island: a defined space within which certain things could happen and certain things could not. From high up, two islands might look much the same. But thousands of lives could be lived within them, each one different.

And anyway, Jack thought, as he ambled from note to note and idea to idea in his head, part of the pleasure of music was its predictability. Most of the songs he loved had a kind of comfort to them. You understood where you were when they started, and you understood pretty much where they would take you. It was reassuring. Along the way, you'd hear something new, maybe something unexpected. But you'd also hear the familiar, the same cluster of chords in each key, and echoes of melodies you'd heard before: little phrases, glimpsed as though from a moving car. They tied the present to the past, those glimpses. They rooted new songs in old traditions.

A bumblebee thrummed close to Jack's ear, then landed on the bench beside him. It crawled an inch one way, then turned and went back again, as though it were looking for something in particular. Jack wondered if it had run out of energy. Sometimes he would find them like that, exhausted, and if there was time he would put some sweetened water down, in the hope they would revive. This one, though, didn't stop for long. Having turned a few circles on the bench, it whirred into life again and disappeared over the top of the house.

Jack had often wondered what songs his great-grandparents might have known, or their great-grandparents before them. What had they sung to each other, or mumbled shyly beneath their breath? What love songs, what laments? Jack had no idea. Whatever they had been, they were not passed down to him. To the best of his recollection, he never heard his grandparents sing a note. The only songs he knew as a child came from his father and mother, and all of those, every one, came from other places.

There was no rich tradition of Shetland songs to speak of. No trove of ballads that reached back across the centuries. There was a handful, that was all. There were scraps and fragments. Jack assumed that when the old language died, a few hundred years ago, almost all of the old songs had died with it, a heritage swallowed by silence. It was an awful thing when you thought about it. So much forever gone. There were plenty of Shetland melodies around, in the form of fiddle tunes, and there were lyrics too, in the form of poems. But it was as if, like secret lovers at a dance, the two had stood apart, gazing at each other from across the hall.

Perhaps because of this very absence, this silence, the songs that had surrounded Jack as a child — songs from Kentucky, from Texas, from Tennessee — had never felt foreign or out of place to him. Jack's father had listened to Jimmie Rodgers and to Johnny Cash, and most of all to Hank Williams. He would play the same albums, the same songs, over and over, until Jack knew those voices as well as he knew his own. But it wasn't just his father. Country music was everywhere in Shetland back then. Whenever people sang, whenever someone picked up a guitar and strummed, it was always country. It was as though, lacking a song tradition of their own, Shetlanders had simply adopted one from elsewhere. They had taken it in, welcomed it, and made it feel at home.

From the time that Jack was first conscious of the world around him, music had been part of it. As much a part — as *tangible* a part — as the walls of the house behind him, and the pitch of the land ahead. It had filled him up, become a kind of vocabulary and a kind of company. He thought in melodies as often as in images; he thought in verses as much as in sentences.

Jack stood to stretch his legs, and walked the length of the vegetable patch, then beyond, to the scrubby grass at the far corner of the garden. There were raspberry bushes there, which had been planted by his mother. He could remember her pride still when the first of the fruits ripened, a little bowl of them set on the kitchen table one evening after dinner. She had waited until Jack and his father had each placed one on their tongues before she reached out herself. Now there were several bushes here. It was hard to tell how many, the stems and suckers were so densely entwined. Jack loved them, despite their disorder. He loved their tenacity and their generosity. He loved the sweet tart fruit that still grew in stubborn abundance.

Just behind the bushes, by the shed, a fence post was loose, and he put his hand on top to check if it was getting worse. It was. The wood was held in place now only by the wire to which it was attached. Jack sighed. The fence, in theory, was Andrew's responsibility, the crofter, but Jack found it was often quicker to deal with things himself. Old Andrew would have been here like a shot if something needed to be done, but Young Andrew usually had other things to be getting on with.

It was one of those afternoons when the whisper of the wind on the hill became entangled with the sounds of the birds: the frantic rapture of the skylarks, the whirring of a snipe, and the wren, down there at the corner of the shed, with his neat flourish of whistles and trills. The whole place was busy, then, with the urgent practicalities of summer.

There was a warmth in the air, or a lack of chill, at least, and the day felt comfortable. Jack leaned against the shed and listened to the wren repeating its refrain. He was thinking about his father, remembering the way he used to sing, at home, unaccompanied. He had a high, lilting voice, at odds with his often gruff manner. If he thought no one was listening, he would slip into whatever tune was in his head at the time. But when he knew his wife or son were there, he had a repertoire he would fall back on. Songs he knew well. And on special occasions, when his wife was particularly pleased with him, or else particularly annoyed, the one he would choose was not his own favourite but hers. She was Kathleen, and she loved – as though he might be singing it just for her – Slim Whitman's version of 'I'll Take You Home Again Kathleen'. It was not a country song, exactly, but nor was it an Irish one, as many people seemed to think. It was American through and through. And in Whitman's hammy cowboy performance, it dwelled somewhere in the vicinity of country.

The first verse arrived in Jack's thoughts, and he followed the lines, not singing them out loud, but letting them play in his mind, hearing them in his father's voice for the first time in years.

*I'll take you home again, Kathleen,*
*Across the ocean wild and wide.*

It was late afternoon, and the sun was high above the ridge. Jack looked up at the bright spot in the clouds behind which it was hiding, and he felt his focus relax. The song, saccharine though it was, filled every bit of attention he possessed.

*And when the fields are fresh and green,*
*I'll take you to your home, Kathleen.*

When those last words faded, and his gaze returned to the grass around his feet, Jack was surprised to find that it was not the sun causing him to squint and blink and rub the back of his hand across his face. His old eyes, blue as forget-me-nots, were swollen with tears.

When Jack stepped into the house again, after an hour or two in the garden, his uninvited guest had entirely slipped his mind. He stopped in surprise when he saw the kitten still perched on the sofa, eyes wide, then went past it to the kitchen. The bowl on the floor had been emptied while he was out. Only a few biscuits were left strewn over the lino. There were crumbs of litter on the floor as well, though the cat had performed quite neatly in that regard. It was housetrained. That was a relief, at least.

'Well, now,' Jack said, in the direction of the living room. 'I'm sorry aboot all this. I bet you're missin home. Missin your mother, maybe.' He paused, feeling daft for speaking out loud. But the kitten looked up as though expecting him to go on.

'We'll get it sorted,' he said, after a moment. 'Find you a nice new home to go to.' The kitten yawned and looked away.

That's enough of that, thought Jack. He boiled the kettle and made himself some tea. He squeezed the bag with his spoon, then scooped it out into a bowl. He took the mug through to the other room.

'Ach,' he said, leaning back in his armchair.

The kitten seemed unnerved with Jack so close, and it retreated to the corner of the sofa. Jack in turn felt oddly shy in front of the cat, as if the creature might be passing judgement on him. Ridiculous, he knew, but indisputable. He wasn't sure whether to continue talking, or just to ignore it.

He set the mug down on the floor beside him, stretched his feet out, ever so slowly, then pressed Play on the remote control. The sound of a mandolin sliced into the room, and the kitten's ears twitched. Jack turned the volume down low, out of respect.

'This is an auld song,' he said. 'Een of my favourites.'

His right foot tapped in time to the 'Kentucky Waltz'. Not Bill Monroe's original, but the Osborne Brothers' version: a little slower and a little sweeter, Jack thought. He closed his eyes to listen.

# THE HURT & THE HEATHER

The birds on the hillside used to sing for me
The dawn used to call out your name
Our love used to fill me like the incoming tide
Now just the hurt & the heather remain

There was ~~sunshine~~ nothing but sunshine ~~all around us~~ on the day we first met
It ~~felt like~~ seemed it never could rain
There was light all around us, I'll never forget I cannot
Now just the hurt & the heather remain

~~broke~~ my best? ~~yet too~~
I tried like hell to love you so well
Then yes I tried it again
But it was more than I could do
~~Just~~ To keep hold of you
Now just the hurt & the heather remain

On the day that you left me you wished me
(all) the best
And you know that I wish you the same
But wishes won't help me can't and /when
the best has long gone
And just the hurt & the heather remain

# the home

## 1959–1960

Sonny Paton and Kathleen Anderson married on a Saturday morning in April, and for the duration of the service the rain never ceased. Like pebbles hurled from the sky, it clattered on the roof of the chapel at Treswick, the long boards and beams above the wedding party's heads shuddering in the downpour. The minister had to raise his voice to a modest yell, but those closest to the door still could not make out the vows. There were some among the small crowd in attendance who heard in that incessant rain a chorus of applause for this joyful occasion, and there were others who heard in it an omen. Most, though, thought nothing of the weather. It was Shetland, and it was raining.

The general consensus within the community was that both Sonny and Kathleen had made fine choices. They had picked wisely. Sonny was a sensible young man. Hard working, too. He didn't have much to show for himself, but he was hardly alone in that. And there were rumours about his savings. He had not been profligate with his

Salvesen wages, that was for certain. Sonny was no great talker, and was neither the life nor the soul of any party. He could be moody, and it was mentioned by a few that he harboured a temper. But better that, most thought, than a man who drinks himself senseless, a man who spends whatever he's got, a man who doesn't know what matters. Sonny was older, perhaps wiser, than his years.

Kathleen, conversely, was a lightsome woman. She laughed easily, and she made others laugh in turn. She had the necessary skills, too, the practicality, the adaptability, the patience required to keep a home. She wasn't much of a knitter, her mother said – her mind had a tendency to stray – and the clothes she made were fit for family, not for sale. But she knew how to mend and make-last. She was well-liked, admired even, and Sonny was not the only man who had hoped to make her his wife. He was just the first to ask.

The asking had happened on the day after his return from the whaling, when he had scrubbed his skin twice over until it smouldered red. He didn't give himself time to cultivate doubts, he just set off on foot towards her parents' house, four miles to the south, his breakfast still heavy in his stomach. It was her mother he met first, in the yard in front of the cottage, and after their pleasantries were done, Sonny explained his intentions. The woman nodded, offering no opinion on the matter, and pointed her thumb towards the house.

Kathleen was surprised by the question, and no wonder. She had known Sonny since they first were at school, and though the previous summer they had spent some time together, always with friends, he had given no indication of his feelings towards her. Yet here he was, not on bended knee exactly, but with a look of pleading on his face that told her just how serious he was. They took a walk, out along the road, towards the sea, then sat together on adjacent rocks. Kathleen knew that she would need a reason to turn him down, as much as she would need one to accept. She listened to him talk about his time away, his eagerness to settle, to make a home. He in turn listened to her speak, and then, for a few moments, they sat in silence, just looking at the waves. It was the ease of that silence that convinced her. She said yes. With one condition. She wouldn't rush. She made him wait the best part of a year to marry. But she said yes.

Together, they were a moderately handsome couple, a fine match indeed, and as they left the chapel that spring afternoon, their neighbours, their friends, their family were happy. This was a splendid day, despite the torrential rain. In seconds, as they paused on the uneven stone steps outside, Kathleen's lace shawl, made by her grandmother, and fine enough to be drawn through her wedding ring, became as lank and as damp as a frond of kelp.

The couple stayed in Hamar for the first time that night, but they did not stay there alone. The house and croft belonged to Kathleen's grand-uncle, Tom, whose wife had died in childbirth four decades earlier, and whose daughter, having survived that awful event, did not survive the bout of influenza that struck on her fifth birthday. The two of them, mother and daughter, were buried in the Treswick kirkyard, side by side, but their names were never spoken in the house at Hamar. Tom was known to be a melancholy man at times, which was hardly a surprise. But he was fond of Kathleen, and he was glad to offer her a home. The house and land would belong to her when he died, he said, and until then, they all would share it. He and Sonny would work the croft together.

Sonny had mixed feelings about this arrangement. His pride was mighty, and the reek of charity was obnoxious to him. Tom's generosity fostered, for many months, a smouldering resentment in the younger man, as if this gift, this kindness, were a debt held over him. But proud as he was, Sonny was not a fool. The house, the land: they were hope, they were a future. And anyway, the couple were hardly alone in living with a relative; many others did the same. They had few options, and this was by far the best of them.

Tom gave up his bedroom, the only one in Hamar at that time. From the day of the wedding until the day he died, he slept in the living room, either on the sofa, beneath a woollen blanket, or else sitting up in his chair, as close to the fire as the season demanded. He seemed content with this arrangement, never bemoaning the loss of privacy or space. He was glad of Kathleen's company, and glad to be useful to her. Even if his grand-niece's new husband could be a damn pain sometimes.

The two of them bickered, Tom and Sonny. Like spiteful siblings, they argued, disagreeing over the best way to carry out almost any task, from fixing a fence to butchering a pig. Mostly, in those first months, they worked apart, only coming together on the croft when more than one pair of hands was required. It was not unusual – especially on those occasions – for them to fall out so completely that they refused to speak to each other for days, communicating only via Kathleen. She was, at such times, both conduit and conciliator, talking the men down from their rage, urging them towards common ground. Patient though she was, their pettiness exhausted her. She missed, then, the good-natured clamour of her childhood home: her brother and sister, both older and married now themselves, and her mother, a widow since the war, but a woman who never let an opportunity to laugh pass her by. Within the vexed silences that Tom and Sonny between them constructed, that childhood home could seem very far away indeed.

By early spring the following year, though, things between the men were beginning to improve. A quiet respect – for Tom's great knowledge of this place and what it needed; for Sonny's persistence and strength – subdued their rancour. And the arthritis that clenched Tom's hands, that raised hard knolls upon his knuckles, convinced him, after all, that Sonny's help was more than just assistance. The younger man was needed.

The croft was not enough for the three of them, of course. It offered food, but no money to speak of. Kathleen worked odd hours here and there, cleaning at the manse in Treswick when the minister's housekeeper was indisposed, which she often seemed to be, or helping her cousins, who sold knitwear by mail order. Kathleen sewed on labels, folded the scarves and ganzies and packaged them up to be posted, leaving her cousins to concentrate on the making.

Tom, whose ability to repair almost any engine he encountered seemed not so much self-taught as innate, continued to do so whenever he was asked, though the ache in his hands made this excruciating at times. Some afternoons, when he'd spent hours dissecting a neighbour's tractor, then putting it back together, he would sit in the garden with his cracked and oil-blackened fingers in a bowl of warm water, easing them back to life again. Sometimes he took money for this work. Sometimes, he was paid in gratitude or in offers of reciprocation that he rarely took up.

Of the three residents at Hamar, Sonny was the one most often away from home. His labour was in demand, his doggedness respected. In the summer, he spent days, and sometimes nights, on his uncle's boat, fishing for herring. On those short trips, he thought often of the Antarctic. He imagined himself back on the catcher or the factory ship, back amid the blood and the stink. And he was always glad to return home.

They were just about comfortable, then, the three of them, no more or less secure than most of their neighbours. They had a place to live, from which no one could evict them. They had food on their table, much of which had been reared or grown on the croft, or else caught by Sonny. Theirs was not an unusual or especially disagreeable living arrangement, though the house did feel small when all three of them were indoors. At such times, it was impossible to avoid each other, and Kathleen would find herself longing for space.

And then three became four.

# 4

Jack did not like driving. It always seemed to him an activity that demanded just a little more concentration and skill than he was able to offer. Beyond the few miles of road he knew best, and on which he travelled almost every day, much of his time behind the wheel was spent clenched, primed for disaster. In fact, Jack had never had an accident while driving. Not even close. But his good luck in that regard thus far, he thought, made it even more likely that he was due one any day. He was alert to that possibility, always, and so drove at a speed that he considered to be safe, and that other motorists considered to be exasperating. He was used to being overtaken.

It was raining that morning as he drove towards Lerwick, down the steep road into the Weisdale valley, past Whiteness, then up again, winding left then right then left, to the top of the hill above Tingwall. His wipers were slapping back and forth, and he'd slowed to a pace that would qualify as unhurried even by his own standards. Wet roads and poor visibility were a high-risk combination.

The view changed entirely at that turning, and between wipes of the windscreen Jack could see the narrow runway of Tingwall Airport, and just above it, on the old road, the cattery. He had called them that morning to say he'd be dropping by with a stray kitten, and they had politely informed him that he was mistaken. They were not a cat shelter, they said, but a commercial cattery. In fact, the woman explained, there *was* no cat shelter. Not any more. The Cats Protection folk could help him find a new home for the kitten if he wanted, but he would have to hold on to it in the meantime, since there weren't enough people willing to foster. When Jack tried to explain the situation, and why it would be best if he could just hand the animal over to someone else, the woman sounded sceptical. 'Why don't you keep it for a few days, then decide?' she said. 'You might enjoy it.'

So that was that.

The sky was clearing just a little as Jack came down the North Road into Lerwick, past the petrol stations, the power station, the ferry terminal. He turned right, towards the supermarket at the other side of town. There was a cafe there, beside the water, and the thought of coffee, maybe cake, would make his time in the shop less tiresome.

Shopping in town was a chore. More so than cleaning, than paperwork – what little of that he had to do. More so even than filling potholes in the road. Jack found the supermarket a stressful and exhausting place. Too many people, too much choice. He had his list made up in advance, and so would set off with his trolley as purposefully as

68

possible, steering first through the fruit and vegetable aisle, then on to the meat. But it was never that simple. The word 'butter' in his notebook meant close to nothing when faced with four shelves of salted, unsalted, organic, local, Scottish, geographically-undefined, spreadable, unspreadable, and any number of other possible options. They made Jack's head spin. And then there was the order of things. Each time he came here, he wrote out his list in the order in which the items were located in the shop, to the best of his recollection. That made things faster, more efficient. Except the shop kept moving around. One month the cornflakes would be in aisle three, and the next they were at the other side of the store. He'd be standing in front of a wall of disposable nappies that ought to have been somewhere else, wondering whether to progress down the aisle or progress down the list.

He was an old buffoon, that was the truth of it. An unworldly man who couldn't be trusted with a task as simple as shopping. That's what he repeated to himself as he paused in the alcohol aisle and picked out a bottle of Maker's Mark whiskey. 'Silly auld fool,' he muttered, beneath his breath. Except, he wasn't really that old.

As he turned his cart towards the next aisle, a man stopped him, and Jack scrambled for his name. Billy, Barry, Bobby? He couldn't recall.

'Hi aye, Jack,' the man said. 'How's things?'

Jack nodded. Maybe it was someone he'd known at school? 'No bad,' he said. 'Same as always. And you?'

'Ach, same same. Knees givin me bother, but aside from that, survivin.'

Jack still didn't know the identity of this man, which left him nowhere to go, conversationally, aside from the obvious. 'Terrible rain this morning,' he said. 'Like a monsoon it was.'

The man shrugged. 'Fine now, though,' he replied, and turned towards the window, through which a narrow band of blue sky was visible.

'Huh,' Jack said, with genuine surprise.

Jack often found conversations to be difficult and unsatisfying, but this was a particularly taxing example. Panic squeezed him as he tried to think of something else to say, and failed. And when the man nodded a farewell, and went off in search of bananas, Jack felt relief at first, then regret, then self-judgement. It didn't please him to be so poor at what others found easy.

Then he remembered. Birnie. John Birnie. That's where the mix-up with the Bs had come from. John Birnie, whose brother had been Jack's colleague when he worked at the airport. Ach, well. That's that.

The queue for the checkout was short. It took only a few moments to get outside again and dump the shopping in the boot of his car. The sky was entirely clear now, and Jack took his coat off, left it on the driver's seat, then strolled across the car park towards the cafe. How quickly things change, he thought to himself. How quickly things change.

He ordered a cappuccino and a fancy sandwich. Steak, cheese, salad. He sat beside the window – the cafe was mostly window, with the sea just a few metres away – and stretched his legs out beneath the table. He sighed, relaxed. It was still early for lunch, and the cafe was quiet, just a few couples nearby, and a group with children in the adjacent room. The couple nearest Jack were both clad in branded outdoor clothing: light rain jackets, walking trousers, boots. Tourists.

A girl in her teens brought Jack's coffee, accompanied by a smile and a cheerfulness that seemed so heartfelt, so radiant, that Jack couldn't help but beam in return.

'I hope you enjoy it,' the girl said, as she set the mug down in front of him.

'I'm sure I will,' he replied. 'Thank you!'

Jack did not harbour the disdain for young people that some of his contemporaries seemed to hold. Instead, he felt something like envy towards them, and something like concern. If he could choose to be young again, he probably would. But he knew, as well, how easily cheer could be knocked out of you. How forcefully. A wave of compassion for the girl broke over him, and, unsure of what to do with that feeling, he looked out of the window.

At the water's edge, an otter appeared, first as a suddenness, a movement, then a shape, as the sleek brown body hauled itself out and onto the seaweed-smothered rocks. At no point was it entirely distinct from those rocks or that weed or that water. It seemed built of all three, never less than half-hidden.

Jack saw otters on his walks now and again, and he'd seen them here before as well. Several times. But he'd never lost that lurch of excitement when one materialised in front of him. Just as when he saw whales, which happened more and more these days, he always felt the urge to tell someone, to share the surprise and the delight.

He looked around. The couple in the fancy outdoor gear were just getting up to leave. He figured they would want to know – they were tourists, after all – but he couldn't bring himself to say anything. And when the girl came back with his food and another smile, he didn't tell her either. She probably saw them all the time. Or else she didn't care.

The otter sprawled on the rock, writhing in the weed as Jack chewed his sandwich in silence. He felt a particular kind of disappointment at the fact that, when words were needed, he could not locate them, yet when there was something he wanted to share he had nobody to tell. It was not a new disappointment, it was an old one, and it returned to him like a weathered stone in his stomach.

If anyone had asked Jack whether he was lonely – which, naturally, they wouldn't – he would have said no. He would have grunted the word and shaken his head, as though the question were worth no more consideration than that. And it would not have been untrue. Jack was so used to his own company, so used to the absence of others in his days, that loneliness was not the state in which he dwelled. He didn't often yearn for other people's presence, and nor did he experience aloneness as discomfort. Some, perhaps, would have thought of him as stoic, but since Jack's circumstances did not feel to him like hardship – at least not ordinarily – that wouldn't be right either.

His equanimity in the face of solitude, though, was not absolute. Jack was human after all. He had aches and pangs and indiscriminate longings. And there were times –

evenings, mostly, though it could linger for days, or even weeks – when he felt wracked by hunger for what he didn't have, for what he'd never had: intimate company, companionship, reciprocal love. He knew these things from books and from songs, and at one time, perhaps, they had felt almost within reach. Now, he was conscious of their absence, even when that absence didn't cause him pain.

This quiet undercurrent of longing, which could rise and surge to the surface at times, was connected, Jack knew, in complicated ways, to his love of music. The passion he felt – the intense, bodily passion – for certain songs. The way that melodies could feel like company, could move and amuse and console. These were connected. Certainly, they were.

So too was his writing.

It was not the same as being in love, to write a song about love. Jack knew that. And it was not the same as losing love, to write a song about heartbreak. But Jack also knew, or thought he knew, that it was not as different as people might believe. To love was an act of imagination. It was to create possible futures, to build new and better selves. When love ended, those futures and those selves were what was lost. Jack knew something of loving from writing love songs. And he knew something of heartbreak, too.

While he would never say that he was lonely, Jack might admit, if pressed, that he was sometimes lonesome. He had always preferred that word. It seemed to him both more potent and less painful. More romantic, less desperate. It was a word he only ever sang, never spoke aloud. And no word, surely, was more deeply embedded in country music.

There were many things, Jack knew, about which a country singer might feel lonesome: drinking too much, getting old, leaving home, missing home, being at home and wanting to be somewhere else, being alone, being with the wrong person, a loved one cheating, a loved one drinking too much, a loved one leaving, a loved one dying, a dog dying, nothing in particular, trains.

Jack could not relate to the last item on this list, though it was by no means an uncommon cause of lonesomeness, if country songs were to be believed. He had travelled by train only a few times in his life, and never very far. But he had seen them, at rest and in motion, on screen and in real life, and they seemed to him no more lonesome-making a form of transportation than, say, a car.

There was symbolism there, he understood: sprawling metaphorical roots. Trains represented freedom, especially to those for whom freedom was out of reach. They represented infinite elsewheres to those who were stuck in one place. They represented progress, welcome or not. Jack knew all that. He could appreciate it, understand it, but he couldn't *feel* it. Whenever he heard a song about a train, he would imagine the first service south out of Aberdeen in the early morning, when he'd just stumbled, bleary-eyed, off the ferry. He would imagine metal refreshment carts, with bad coffee and damp sandwiches. He would imagine standing by the toilet door, as he once did for two hours straight, in a hot, overcrowded carriage that stank of sweat and – each time that door was opened – worse.

In songs, it was often the whistle of a train that was the trigger for lonesomeness. It was the sound not the sight that

74

did it. Jack had heard recordings of that sound, and he had to admit there was something mournful about it, something that seemed in harmony with country music. It reminded him somewhat of a ship's whistle, or a foghorn – a sound that once had been familiar to him, but which he hadn't heard now in years, since they all were switched off.

To Jack, a foghorn was as potent a symbol as a train, since it represented not freedom but safety, or danger, depending on how you thought about it. Where a train's whistle could induce a longing for other places, a foghorn, like a light-house, was a warning, a reminder that land and sea could kill you, given the chance. That great, lonesome bellow was a reaching out into the perilous unseen. But so far as Jack could recall, there were no country songs about foghorns.

Across the carpeted expanse of the living room at Hamar, Jack and the kitten eyed each other. Over the course of several days, a change had come over the animal. Its mood had lightened, its fear diminished. Now, when Jack entered the room, the cat didn't watch him with concern, but instead hopped off its cushion to greet him, elongating itself into an enormous yawn, paws outstretched. It would scuttle, then, into the kitchen, where it would gaze at the empty food bowl on the floor, then up at Jack, then back again at the bowl.

'Miaow,' it would say, high-pitched and pathetic. 'Miaow.'

A change had come over Jack, as well, and he found himself smiling at these exchanges, amused by the demands the animal made of him, and the confidence with which it now roamed the house.

That evening – its fourth at Hamar – the kitten and Jack were sitting down to a meeting of sorts, a summit, in which neither party could quite comprehend the other.

'You'll need a name, I suppose,' said Jack, who had come round to the idea of keeping this creature more easily than he would ever have predicted. 'I'll hae to call you somethin.'

The kitten twitched its ears in response. Then it waited.

Jack scanned the room for inspiration. A musical name would be appropriate. Something resonant and strong. He searched the spines of the CDs beside him, looking for ideas. There were many. He would need a list, so he could narrow it down.

He opened the notebook that was lying on the coffee table, and tore a page from the back. The pen was on the floor beside the fire. The kitten had been chasing it earlier, batting with one paw, then leaping after it as if it were alive, and the lid, now, was missing. Jack checked the ink, then stood facing the wall, reading, writing.

For a brief minute, he considered the simple solution of naming the cat after Kitty Wells. It was a name that, in this case, was also just a label, and that appealed to him. But thinking it through, he realised it was impossible. He could not imagine ever saying the word Kitty out loud without feeling completely ridiculous. Even if no one else ever heard him.

He crossed it out. So what then? The list shrank.

Patsy? Possible, but no.

Tammy? Preferable, but no.

Reba? Wynona? No.

Connie? Wanda? Tanya? No, no, no.

76

Dolly? Absolutely not. No matter how fond he was of her songs.

After much consideration and much crossing out, Jack settled on a shortlist of two: Emmylou and Loretta.

He was tempted, sorely, by the former. There were few voices he loved as much as Emmylou Harris's voice. In his teens, he'd been besotted by her, had bought each of her albums on the day of its release, had listened, captivated, had gazed at their covers in a state of bafflement and desire. It was hard for him to believe that such a human could actually exist in the world. And yet, there she was, real to his eyes and his ears. Real to his heart, too, which stung with the knowledge that, for him at least, she might as well not have been.

He got over his crush eventually, more or less, but he was still infatuated by her voice. There was such richness to it, and such generosity. She could sound youthful and wise at once; world-weary and yet ready for anything. She cast a kind of angelic light over every song on which she sang. And that was a whole lot of songs.

The kitten, though, did not cast angelic light. There was a sweetness to her sometimes, Jack thought, but mostly when she was sleeping. Much as he liked the name, then, and much as he would happily have used it more often, Emmylou just didn't seem right.

Loretta, on the other hand, well, that name spoke of mettle and sass, of gutsiness and defiance. It was going too far, perhaps, to suggest the cat might have much in common with Loretta Lynn, but somehow the name seemed to fit her more comfortably. It seemed like it might just work.

He said the word aloud – 'Loretta' – and the kitten, who

had long since fallen asleep, raised one ear and one eyelid, just for a second. She looked at Jack, and for him that clinched it.

The kitten was Loretta, and the kitten would stay.

# THE LIGHTHOUSE

There's an old moon on the ocean ~full?~
Reflected from above
There's an old song on the radio
Do you remember 'Faded Love'?
There's ~another~ an old storm between us
~Though we've weathered worse before~
But it's not felt ~like~ this before.
~As~ you look at to the ~strong~ lighthouse
On the unforgiving shore

If you're passing by I ~~ will light your way
So you can go alone
But if you're lost I will lead you home

Though we're here inside the same room
You feel so far from me
You're like a ship ~afloat~ alone, adrift,
Upon that ~aching~ endless sea
But you know that I still love you, as
I've loved you ~all along~ / for so long
I just wish that I could understand
What it is that ~t did~ I've done wrong

79

◁ If you're passing by . . .

Bridge:

There's danger all around (us) and
There's nowhere we can hide
Here just a pair of lonely lovesone fools souls
In peril upon on the tide

—

There's no point in pretending
That everything's okay
There's no point in just lingering drifting hanging on
If you're not going to stay
darling
But you know that when if you need to
you can always count turn to on me
cos I'm as steady as that the lighthouse
That looks out on the sea

C And If you're passing by . . .

# the extension

## 1960

From the moment Kathleen first told him she was pregnant to the moment the last block was laid, the last paint applied, and the cot brought in to the brand new bedroom, Sonny hardly paused. The news – welcome though it was – for him was principally a call to action. Something had to change. He conferred with Tom that very evening, and set out to plan an extension to the house, sketching it on paper first, then firming up the details as the days went on.

The rumour Kathleen had heard when she first told people of their engagement was true: Sonny did have money in the bank (he had never told her this before, and she had never asked). It wasn't a great deal – just a safety net, he called it – but it was enough to pay for the materials, and what specialist labour was required to get the new rooms built. The rest Sonny would manage himself, with help from Tom and from the many neighbours who owed them assistance.

An extra bedroom, a proper bathroom, a bigger kitchen: that was what they needed. A full extension out the back of the house, into the garden. The cottage would become square, more or less, not quite doubling the space, but not far off it either. Sonny explained it to Kathleen, so she could imagine how it might look. He laid the plans on the table, answered her questions, and then he set to work.

For Kathleen, her husband's toil seemed an act of the utmost devotion, and she watched the building emerge with a deep and unexpected sense of wonder. She saw the foundations being poured, the surface of the concrete trembling like porridge as it rose. She saw the first blocks laid, and the outline of their new half-home appear. In those months of construction, Kathleen looked at her husband with a fervour and an admiration that was new to her. Even on nights when he returned grumpy and frustrated, when he came to bed without washing the cement from his hair, when he tramped mud or sawdust across the living-room floor, she adored him, desired him, needed him. She felt, for the first time in their marriage, a sense of abundance − not material abundance, but an overflowing of affection and of hope. These rooms in which they soon would live, Kathleen believed, would be a physical embodiment of Sonny's love for her, and for their child. The fact that the extension, as it took shape, proved to be utilitarian in appearance, verging on ugly, dampened that belief hardly at all.

As the house at Hamar grew, so too did Kathleen. Her belly swelled in a kind of harmony with the new rooms. The skin at her middle was already tightening when the work began, and by the time the roof went on, the felt stretched out and nailed down, she was visibly round, her stance altered, her pace slowed.

The change in his wife's body spurred Sonny on. He worked harder, staying out late into the evenings. It was May by then, and the nights were short. If he needed, he could stop at 10 p.m. and start again before anyone else was awake. Often, that's exactly what he did. Driven by a deadline that could be neither altered nor precisely identified, he wore himself out with working. His face became drawn, the food he swallowed each mealtime not quite enough to sustain the energy he was expending. He stopped shaving, to hide the thinness of his cheeks.

Help came readily then, as neighbours saw the end approaching. Old debts and favours were repaid in full. On a day in June, a hole was hammered from the hallway into the extension, then another, larger, hole joined the old kitchen to the new one. Dust billowed everywhere, covering all they owned, as the two halves of the house came together. Everyone cheered as it settled, then Kathleen set to work cleaning up.

Those last weeks were hard. The precision required to finish the rooms, to cut timbers for window trims and wall panelling, to lay floors, to fit cupboards, was almost beyond Sonny by then. Some days he seemed half delirious with exhaustion, laughing one minute then yelling the next. He made mistakes, cursed, and made the same mistakes again. Tom would spend a few hours with him, until he could suffer it no longer, then he'd return to help Kathleen, letting her rest whenever she needed. Tom had looked upon the changes to his home with real pleasure, at first, impressed by Sonny's dedication, and by the undeniable improvements it was bringing. Now, with the birth almost upon them, he was growing anxious, desperate for the work – and the pregnancy – to be over.

There came a day in early August when they knew, all of them, that the baby was late. Kathleen, by then, was struggling to get around, and neighbours brought food for the family each evening. Tom, though he had fed himself perfectly well for decades, had now become next to useless, consumed as he was by old fears. His fretting and fidgeting got on everyone's nerves. He would watch Kathleen as if she might be about to disappear, and she found herself providing him with reassurance, time and time again. The three of them, each in their own way, were fragile.

Perhaps it was the air of festivity in Shetland that week that did it, bestowed by the presence of Queen Elizabeth and her family, the first British monarch ever to visit the islands. Or perhaps it was relief, the sheer elation that the work was now over and the extension was complete. Or perhaps, even, it was the smell: the sharp stink of white spirit that filled the house. Sonny was cleaning paintbrushes in the new kitchen, the white wall panels still tacky around him, when he heard his wife cry out. Tom, who had insisted that Kathleen should give birth in the hospital in Lerwick rather than at home, and who had been ready for this moment for more than a fortnight, ran so quickly to the car – borrowed for this purpose – that he almost forgot to wait for his passengers.

They came home, all of them, eight days later, and it was hard to say who among them was most tired. Tom seemed shellshocked, unable quite to trust that everything had gone to plan, that mother and baby were both well. He and Sonny had chosen to stay with an old friend of his in Lerwick throughout, but Tom had lain awake most nights, his heart racing, his panic ever-present. Sonny, meanwhile, was barely more than a shadow. After months of working himself to the bone and beyond, he could hardly hold himself upright. He had within him a swelling pride and delight at the fact of his new son, but it wasn't enough to keep him going. When they got in the door of the cottage, the two men sat down and fell, almost immediately, to sleep. And so it was Kathleen, whose body no longer felt like her own, whose pain was everywhere, who took the child to the new bedroom and laid him inside his cot. For a few minutes he wriggled, moved his head from side to side as if he might be about to cry, and then closed his eyes. Kathleen watched over him until she was sure he was sleeping, then she set a pillow on the floor, and lay down alongside him.

The house was quiet. The room, still almost empty, felt strange to her. She looked up at the ceiling, her eyes tracing its edges as if to imprint the shape of this space in her mind. She listened to the flutters and sighs of her son's breath. She longed, too, for sleep, but her body wouldn't take her there. She was alert.

Kathleen sat back up, looked through the wooden bars at the tiny creature that was her son. He was, she thought, the most beautiful thing ever to have existed, the most perfect creation on earth. *Her* creation. Hers and Sonny's. Just to look at him was intoxicating. She could stare and stare and stare, and never tire of him.

She imagined the life he might have, this child, all that he might do in the world. Oh, it was just the most extraordinary thing to have the future in front of you like this, to reach out and lay a hand upon it, to love it, and to be loved by it in turn. Her son could be anyone. He could do anything.

Kathleen woke an hour later, on the bare bedroom floor. She could not remember having lain down again, but there she was, her head on the pillow, her arms aching from the hard boards beneath her. Her boy, in the cot, yowling to be fed.

The residents of Hamar came together the next day to decide on a name for the child. Tom expressed no firm opinion on the matter; it was not his decision to make, but he wanted to be there when it was chosen, and to hear the name spoken for the first time.

Kathleen had three suggestions. There was William, her late father's name; James, her grandfather's; and there was Tom. Sonny shook his head as she spoke each of them in turn, though he offered a reason only against the last of these. 'Twa Toms in wan hoose,' he said. 'What happens when I call for the boy? They'll both come runnin.'

'And what would be so wrong wi that?' Tom intervened.

Sonny was quiet for a moment. 'I think our son deserves a grander name,' he said. 'Somethin more . . . heroic maybe.' Sonny had found himself, just as his wife had done, imagining great futures for this tiny child. The momentousness of his birth demanded it.

'Heroic?' Kathleen laughed. 'Do you mean a hero like Hercules or like Hank Williams?' She looked at the sleeping child in her lap and smiled to herself. She wanted to stroke his face, but worried she might wake him.

Sonny did not laugh. 'I thought we could name him after Shackleton,' he said. 'That's what I meant by heroic.'

Kathleen wasn't sure at first if her husband was serious, though he was hardly a man known for his jokes. She looked at him and saw, with dismay, that he was. Sonny's admiration for the explorer was not a surprise. He had recounted Shackleton's adventures in the Antarctic so many times, it was as if those outrageous journeys had been his own. But this, this was ridiculous.

'We canna call the boy *Ernest*, for heaven's sake,' Kathleen said, then lowered her voice. 'He'd be a laughin stock at school.'

Sonny thought about this, and he knew, to his regret, that she was right. He thought a moment longer. 'What aboot Jack, then?' he asked. 'They called Shackleton that sometimes, Cautious Jack. No to his face, mind, but still.'

'Cautious Jack? Are you sure that's the kind of label we want him to grow into?'

'Well, Shackleton rowed across the Antarctic Ocean, climbed over the mountains of Sooth Georgia wi a few metres of rope, and managed to save every one of his men in the process. If that's cautious then I reckon it's a name to be prood of.' Sonny had got himself quite worked up.

Kathleen didn't argue. In fact, she rather liked the name. Plain, but not too common. Solid, dependable, simple. It sounded right in her mouth. She looked at Tom, who had said nothing at all since his own name had been so quickly passed over. He shrugged in response. 'Suits him,' he said, and he meant it.

She looked down again at the sleeping child. Tom was right. It suited him.

'Jack,' she whispered, the decision made. 'Wake up, Jack!'

# 5

When Jack sold his family's croft to Old Andrew, his nearest neighbour at the time, he chose to keep possession of the long stone shed beside the house, in which all of his father's machinery and tools were stored. There were a number of reasons he opted not to sell the building – and Andrew, for his part, didn't try to change Jack's mind, though a crofter can always do with more sheds.

One reason was pragmatic. While most of what had been stored in there was of no use whatsoever to Jack, since he would no longer be keeping sheep, making silage, or repairing tractors, he still intended to live a moderately practical life. He had gardening tools, shovels, painting materials, a wheelbarrow, and he needed a place to store them. The shed was far too big for his requirements, but what did that matter?

Another reason was, for want of a better word, senti-mental. The shed had been his father's, and before that, his great-grand-uncle Tom's, and when Jack thought of them, often as not, he thought of them inside its walls. He thought of them in boilersuits, hunched over the workbench, making, mending. The idea of someone else in there, banging around, or even just storing sheep feed, was uncomfortable to him. He didn't like it one bit.

Jack opened the door on the front wall, and stooped to go inside. The air was cool and stale. It smelled of stone and petrol. He reached up to pull the string beside the entrance and the strip lights above cluck-cluck-clucked into life. The room was exposed. It was sparse and simple: a concrete floor and bare granite walls. Along most of one side was the workbench, and on the other were narrow stalls in which, until Jack's early teens, two cows had spent each winter. At the far end, a wall had been removed by his father and replaced by double doors, so the tractor could be driven in and out. The tractor, though, was long gone. Jack had sold it almost as soon as his parents died, in order to make space for the boat.

The boat was still there – a white fourareen, with top board and gunwales painted royal blue – supported by three wooden trestles. It was called the *Wayfarer*. Jack's father, Sonny, had bought it when Jack was eleven years old. Back then, it was kept by the pier at Treswick, but on the day after Sonny and Kathleen disappeared, it had washed up closer to the house. And though the weather had been calm, and though the boat was intact when it was found, and though Jack's mother almost never accompanied his father on the sea, the *Wayfarer*'s discovery, empty and adrift, had provided an explanation that did not need to be questioned. Everybody knew these things happened, even to a sailor as competent as Sonny. *These things just happened.*

Jack had someone bring the boat back to the house, and it had never left the shed since then. The paint on its sides had puckered and peeled in the damp air. Mice had nested beneath the bottom boards, having gained access up the legs of the trestles.

Perhaps there was something morbid about keeping the vessel on which his parents had spent their last moments, the vessel that had, in a certain sense, killed them. Jack wasn't sure why he held on to it any more, except, what else would he do with it? No one he knew would want it – folk could be superstitious that way – and he wouldn't let a stranger have it either. So here it stayed, just growing old with him.

Jack put a hand on the gunwale, patted the wood, then headed for the work bench. He pulled out a drawer from the metal cabinet below, rummaged, closed it, then opened the next drawer down. He found what he was looking for: a set of little screwdrivers in a plastic wallet, most of which were useless to him. He pulled a pair of spectacles from his shirt pocket – his reading glasses, on which he'd sat the day before – and set them on the bench. He tried first one screwdriver, then another, until he found the one that fitted, turning the tiny screws at the hinge until the wonky leg came off.

He held it up in front of him, and began to massage the metal, trying to bend it back to its original shape. The biggest kink, right in the middle, undid itself easily, but the ends were trickier. Jack laid it down and gently tapped at it with a ball-peen hammer. Now he was getting some-where. It looked almost straight.

He screwed the leg back on, and put the glasses on his face. They weren't right, that was for sure. They sat unevenly on his nose, and the bent leg hooked uncomfortably around his ear. But perhaps they were good enough. He didn't wear them often, after all. His eyes were more or less fine, and he'd bought these – the cheapest he could find in the shop – only because the optician told him he ought to. Sure, the words looked a little clearer when he wore them than when he didn't, but it was marginal. They lived mostly on the arm of his chair, and sometimes, like yesterday, on the seat itself.

As Jack took the glasses off again and held them up, to see if there was anything else he could do, there was a noise, a scuffling from the furthest stall. Once, then twice. He stopped to listen. Nothing, nothing, then another sound.

This shed was full of mice, and there was no point even trying to do anything about that. They could stay, as far as Jack was concerned. Now and again there were rats too, and Jack was less accommodating when it came to those. On one occasion, he'd seen a polecat in here as well, maybe scouting it out for a possible nest site. He'd scared the thing away, then never seen it again.

Given the volume, he assumed it was a rat making the noise this time, though usually they stayed silent when he was around – much more timid than you might imagine. Jack folded the glasses again and put them back in his pocket, then went to take a look, stepping as quietly as he could down the length of the boat, until, from behind the stern, he could see into the stall.

'What in the hell?' Jack said.

The kitten turned to look at him, then turned back, twisted and pounced, grabbing hold of its own tail. It rolled on its back for a second, kicking its legs furiously, then leapt into the air as if shocked by a cattle prod.

'How in the hell did you get in here?' Jack asked, as though an answer might actually come. He'd not yet allowed Loretta out of the house, assuming she would most likely disappear – an outcome he no longer wished for. But here she was.

The kitten continued leaping and spinning, engaged in some kind of game, the rules and objective of which Jack could not even guess. He watched her, his surprise turning to amusement, laughter, delight. He leaned against the stern of the boat.

Finally, Loretta made an error. She jumped onto the lawnmower, slipped on the plastic top and tumbled back to the floor again. Then she stood, raised her tail towards the roof, and padded towards Jack, rubbing her face against his leg. He leant down and scratched her head, ran his hand down the length of her.

'Silly thing,' he said, his voice softening to a whisper. 'Silly, silly thing.'

When he turned for the door, the kitten followed, prancing along behind him all the way to the house, only pausing once to peer into a tussock of long grass, then running to catch up again.

Jack had left the front door lying open.

★   ★   ★

Jack was in his early forties when he realised – and it came to him like that, a realisation, with a sharp and painful clarity – that he would likely never live a life that was significantly different from the one he was living then, the one he was still living now, twenty years later. That realisation had pained him not because he had a strong wish to be doing something else in particular. He didn't. But only because an alternative life, which had once seemed possible, and sometimes desirable, then, as now, was scarcely imaginable.

It wasn't about opportunities, or about doors that had closed – though there were likely some of those. Jack could have packed a bag and set off for the mainland any day. He could have sold his house and bought a flat in a town where no one knew him. It would have been easy enough, practically speaking. But what struck him at that time, forcefully, was the recognition that he never would. The older he got, the harder such a choice became, and, having not taken it in his younger days, the chance that he would do so then, in his forties, or now, in his sixties, was close to nil.

Actually, it wasn't quite true to say that Jack had not taken the chance to leave. In fact, he had. He did. He went. When he was twenty years old, he'd got on the ferry, the *St Clair*, in Lerwick, had sat the whole night in an uncomfortable chair, with his bag and guitar case beside him. It was his first time away from the islands, and he had left on a last-minute whim, with hardly more than a week's warning.

From Aberdeen, where the ferry came in, he took the train to Glasgow, where two of the boys from his class at school were then living. One was finishing college, the other an apprenticeship as an electrician. They rented a big room with two beds in a boarding house just south of the Clyde, and the landlady said that Jack could join them, temporarily, if he slept on the floor. It was cheap, and breakfast was included.

His mother had implored him not to go, not without a plan, a job, something solid to hold on to. But Jack didn't listen. He figured he'd find work of some sort, soon enough, and he figured, too, that he would find music. Maybe even get the chance to play himself. Glasgow was a big city. There would be all kinds of chances. He was naïve, that was true, but any confidence he had was borrowed from his father. Sonny, at that age, had been in the Antarctic killing whales, as he never stopped reminding Jack. To move to a city a few hundred miles from home: that was nothing in comparison.

In those first days in Glasgow, there were times when he would happily have swapped the city for the Antarctic. All those people, all that noise, that thick, fetid air: he had never imagined it could be so awful. Stepping out of the front door in the morning, he would have to stop on the street and adjust to the passing traffic, adjust to the pace of the world around him. He would walk slowly, as far from the kerb as he could, but he never lost the feeling of danger, or of being in everybody's way.

At night, his friends went to the pub around the corner, and a few times Jack joined them. He couldn't afford to drink much, not until he found a job, but it was fine to be there amongst all those people, and to feel the warmth of a beer or two. He refused to take a drink bought by anyone else, in case they expected him to buy in return. He just sipped, drank one for every three that Stuart and Kevin consumed. Then they'd sneak back into the house and up the stairs after closing time, quiet as they were able, and snore until the morning.

Most days, Jack just walked. He walked across the bridge to the centre of the city, walked east to the Necropolis, to Dennistoun, and beyond, walked west to Broomhill and Anniesland. He gravitated towards quieter streets, never planning his route in advance, just striding onwards, then turning left or right when the notion took him. Sometimes he ended up in places where he knew, instinctively, that he ought not to be, where the sense of threat, and of being out of place, was acute. Other times, he stumbled upon things that made him stop and stare. The first time he turned a corner and saw Kelvingrove Museum, he was awestruck. Never before had he seen a building so beautiful. It seemed almost to glow in the afternoon light. He had longed, then, to go inside, but had not done so, fearing the cost. Instead, he walked around it, admiring, then came back again and did the same the next day.

What Jack was supposed to be doing was looking for a job and a better place to live. That was what would allow him to stay in the city. He had enough money to last him a month, six weeks at a stretch, but after that he would have nothing. He knew where the nearest job centre was – he'd seen men go in and out as he walked by – but he never went through the door himself. He didn't know what he wanted to do, that was the thing, and he imagined himself being forced down a coal mine for lack of a better plan. So he stayed away.

In the back of his mind, he might have thought that, with all that walking, he would eventually find himself in the right place at the right time. If he just kept on the move, a job would sooner or later appear in front of him, and he wouldn't be able to miss it. But after three weeks he still hadn't found one.

What he also hadn't found were musicians, or even music – the kind of music he wanted to hear. Sometimes, in the pub, an old fellow would scratch a fiddle or squeeze an accordion, but that was the last thing Jack needed. He could get that, and better, back home. There were clubs too, discos, and the Apollo, where the bigger bands would play. But what he wanted was country music, and he didn't know where to find it. Kevin and Stuart laughed when he asked them, and since he knew no one else in the city, since he didn't have the first clue even where to look, he hit a dead end right away.

In that third week, though, Stuart came home from work one evening with a grin on his face.

'My boss,' he said, when Jack asked him what he looked so cheerful about, 'he's into all that stuff you like. Country and western. He dresses up at the weekend: cowboy shirt, boots, the whole lot. There's a club for it. A music club, for people like you.'

And that was how Jack learned about Glasgow's Grand Ole Opry. It was remarkable, in fact, that he hadn't stumbled across it already, since it was only twenty minutes from the house. He must have walked circles around it over the past few weeks.

He went that very evening – not to go inside, just to look, to check that it was real, that Stuart had been telling the truth. He stood across the road, gazing up at the great illuminated sign, at those three words that carried him across the ocean, all the way to Nashville. He crossed the street, read the notice by the door with the names of the bands that would play that weekend, and he thought that surely he had found his place. He walked back to the house feeling more certain, more settled, than he had since the day he left home.

When he got there, to the boarding house, he barely registered the red-and-white police car sitting outside. He had his hands in his pockets and his head down, and he was humming to himself. He turned the key in the front door, and heard some movement from Mrs McGill's living room on the left. Her door opened, and she stood there looking at him, as if searching for something she couldn't find.

'You poor boy,' was all she said, in the end. 'You poor boy.' Then she stepped aside to let the policeman, hat in hand, give Jack the news. The words he spoke, simple though they were, landed like a shattered pane, something that could not be made sense of or put back together. Just pieces of sound, fragments of meaning. Each of them sharp enough to draw blood. Jack sat on the staircase and looked out of the still-open front door. He looked at the cars passing. A bus. A taxi. He turned back to the policeman.

The next night, he was on his way home again, with his bag and his guitar. Despite a search lasting several days, only his father's boat – battered, but intact – was ever found.

★　★　★

Jack turned the key and put his car into gear. There was an ugly sound, just below the noise of the engine: a kind of rattle, as if a pebble were being thrown around beneath the bonnet. It had started a few weeks back, and had not gone away. Jack didn't know the first thing about cars, but nor did he feel inclined to take it to the garage. It was only a sound after all. Patience, he figured, was the best policy. If he waited, it might just disappear.

He lowered the handbrake and set off at a crawl. It was just after 6 p.m., and he was on his way to work. He'd had macaroni cheese for dinner, and his stomach felt swollen. He adjusted the seatbelt with his left hand.

Had he not been driving so slowly the girl in the middle of the track might have given him a fright. But as it was, and especially given the bright red mackintosh she was wearing, which came all the way down to her knees, he saw her from a long way off. The girl was Vaila, Sarah's daughter, from next door, and as he drew closer Jack smiled to himself. She looked more and more like her mother all the time, he thought. She had seemed to him quite a serious child, ever since she was little. But the capacity to beam was present in her face, as it was in Sarah's.

He expected the girl to step out of the way as he approached, but that was not what happened. She didn't move. Like a stubborn sheep, she stayed put, blocking his route, and since there was no space to drive around her, Jack had to stop. He turned off the engine. The girl approached the car, and he wound down his window.

'You shouldna stand in the road like that,' Jack said. 'It's no safe.'

'I wanted to speak to you,' Vaila told him, as if she hadn't heard what he'd just said. She looked almost solemn.

'Oh,' Jack said. 'What did you want to speak aboot?'

'Your cat,' Vaila replied. 'What's it called?'

Jack laughed, then felt a tingle of embarrassment as he answered. 'She's called Loretta,' he said.

'That's a funny name for a cat.' The girl screwed her face up to emphasise this opinion.

'Is it?'

'Yes.'

'Oh. What are cats supposed to be called, then?'

Vaila seemed pleased to be asked. 'My friend Abigail has a cat,' she said, 'and his name is Fluffy.'

Jack thought about this. 'Hmm,' he said. 'I guess that could be a good name. But my cat isna a fluffy cat, so I called her Loretta instead.'

'What is she like?'

'She's black, wi a bit of white just under her chin.' Jack lifted his head to demonstrate. 'And een of her paws too. She's friendly. She likes sleepin and chasin things. The usual cat stuff, I suppose.'

'Can I come and see her?'

'No, sorry. I'm on my way to work.'

'When will you be back?' Vaila looked frustrated.

'Probably after you go to bed. Eight o'clock maybe.'

'Oh.' Now she was disappointed. 'Can I come tomorrow, then? It's Saturday.'

Jack figured he wasn't going to find an easier route out of this conversation, and so he told her yes. She could come tomorrow. 'But ask your mother first. Dunna come unless she says it's all right.'

Vaila grinned, as if this were the happiest news she could imagine.

'Tell me what's she's called again,' she asked.

'Loretta,' Jack said, pronouncing it as clearly as he could.

She repeated the name four times – 'Loretta, Loretta, Loretta, Loretta' – then she spun around twice on the road, arms outstretched, and ran towards her garden gate. 'See you tomorrow,' she shouted, bounding up the steps to the house.

Jack laughed, then turned the key in the ignition. The rattling sound returned.

# WHEN I TALK
# IN MY SLEEP

I never really said goodbye, I just
    turned & walked away
I didn't mean to be so cruel, but ‡
  I wasn't strong enough to stay
There's years behind me now, a long forgotten way
I've lost more than I ever knew I had
it's the price I had to pay. really?

CHORUS
When I lie in my bed, when I tremble & stir,
When I talk in my sleep, I'm thinking of her
    (rpt)              (?) I'm talking to her.


Some moments never leave me / you
~~They never leave me alone~~  Some failures
                              never fade
Some things were never really there at all
Like notes left unmade
  She's never not been with me, in every
                              place I've lain
I would give everything that I still own
To be in her ~~heart~~ thoughts again

When I lie in my bed ...
                    (rpt)

102

# the happier days

The early years of Jack's life were among the happiest times his great-grand-uncle Tom had ever known. He took to the role of honorary grandparent and childminder with an enthusiasm that nobody – least of all he – had ever anticipated. From the boy's very first week at home there seemed to be a bond between them, an understanding even. Sometimes, when the child lay squalling and inconsolable, Tom would pluck him from his mother's arms and set off, bounce-walking, into the garden or around the house, the baby's head nestled against his shoulder. Screams would turn to sobs would turn to silence. Tom whispered to his chest, describing what he could see, and what he remembered and knew of this place. He told the child about his own life, his childhood here, and about his wife and his daughter, who might have been a mother now herself, had she lived. Jack was the only person, in fact, who Tom ever spoke to about his losses, about the woman and girl he had loved and buried and grieved forever after.

He felt himself lightened by the child's presence. He felt that grief ebb, finally, even as his memories of them remained as vivid as ever.

When Jack spoke his first word – 'mama' or 'Hamar', it was hard to tell – Tom was there to hear it. When he took his first unsteady steps, it was between Kathleen's hands and Tom's, a grin of determination on the infant's face as his fat legs carried him across the carpet, beside the fire.

Sonny never expressed any jealousy over the time that Tom spent with Jack. More than anything, he was grateful that someone else was there to make life easier for Kathleen. It left Sonny more time for the croft – and the croft always needed more time. In truth, his son's first years were of less interest to him than the ones that would come later. He looked forward to working with Jack, to teaching him what he knew, to guiding him towards adulthood. Until then, he was happy to take a back seat and let others lead. Sonny wasn't exactly absent in those years, but nor was he especially present. Parenthood, for him, was largely a hands-off endeavour, as it had been for his own father. He was an observer more than a participant in Jack's first years.

Despite the house being larger than before, Tom never did get his room back. He was content, he said, to stay where he was. He'd grown used to it, and preferred, now, the sofa or the armchair to a bed of his own. And so the new bedroom became Jack's, and when he got up in the night – as he did with some frequency until he was seven years old – he would often not wake his parents at all. He would go no further than the living room, where Tom would make space for him on the sofa. The boy would snuggle in, and soon be back asleep, the grey woollen blanket rising and falling with each of his breaths. Tom would watch over him, until he too was sleeping.

It was the older man, whose time was more his own in those days than either of Jack's parents, who really showed the child that small corner of the world that belonged to him. Almost as soon as he was able, Jack would walk with Tom, trotting alongside him or a few feet behind, checking walls and fences, checking livestock, checking oats and potatoes. Sometimes, when nothing in particular needed to be done, they would walk as far as the sea, taking the long way to the north, around the edge of the high ridge. Then they would turn around and come home.

Between his parents, Jack seemed at first to most take after his mother. He was a jolly child, who laughed freely, and though he was taught to be wary of his father's moods he never seemed fearful. The sense of safety in which he grew was broken only rarely. Jack learned the weight of his father's hand on his backside, and he learned the weight of his mother's too. Her cheer had its limits. Kathleen, by now, was spending much of her time earning money. She had bought a knitting machine. She found herself more suited to that work than she had been to the needles. She could lose hours in front of it each day, her arm cranking back and forth across the wires, as the pattern card clicked onward like paper through a typewriter, and the garment drooped towards the floor. Jack could be a nuisance as a toddler, getting in amongst the wool, trying to stay close to his mother. More than once, frustrated, she lashed out. She knew exhaustion then as she had never known it before.

She could not imagine how they ever would have coped without Tom.

In the evenings sometimes, after Jack had gone to sleep and the dinner dishes were cleaned and put away, Kathleen would sit on the stool in the corner of the living room beside the record player. Tom would be in the armchair, Sonny on the sofa, and they would talk over what work needed doing on the croft, what the weather would bring tomorrow, what new plans needed to be made. Kathleen would take a record from its sleeve – Slim Whitman or Jim Reeves – and turn the volume down low. Barely more than a whisper. She would close her eyes and focus in on the voice, feel herself lifted and carried by the melody, by the sentiment, until, neither quite awake nor quite asleep, it was if the songs were her own daydreams, as if they had been born, in that moment, inside her. When the needle reached the end and the hiss roused her, she would be drawn back again, to the sound of her husband and Tom, and to the thought of her son in his bed in the next room. Those few moments, for her, could be as restorative as a full night's sleep.

When he was three years old, Jack began to seem uneasy with adults from beyond the household. Even with his grandparents, his aunts and uncles, whom he saw only rarely as they lived several miles beyond Treswick, he could be shy. His usual ease would be overtaken by a quiet discomfort, as if he were suffering from stage fright. He would retreat to a corner or a doorway to watch.

Tom, at first, took it upon himself to iron out this crease in the boy's character. He was becoming more sociable in his old age, and he would take Jack with him on his visits to friends and neighbours. He thought that, with a bit of a nudge, and without his parents around, Jack might just come out of his shell. But the further they were from the house, the closer he would stick. Often, Tom would be sat in the warmth of a neighbour's kitchen, cups of tea on the table, with Jack beneath him on the floor, clinging to the frayed cuff of his trouser leg, hidden from view.

Once or twice on those occasions, Tom gently mocked the boy for his refusal to perform. 'Mute as a post,' he might say. 'Silent as a stone.' The adults would laugh among themselves, then return to their conversation, forgetting for a time that Jack was even there. Afterwards, always, Tom would feel an intense and painful regret for his disloyalty. Why had he made a fool of the child like that? Why had he drawn attention to his silence? As they walked home together, Tom would pull the boy close, a hand on his shoulder, and vow never to laugh at him again.

It is rarely a satisfying game, to pick a person apart, to seek causes for every effect. Jack's shyness, his reluctance to expand the world beyond the stone dykes of Hamar, was not inherited from either of his parents. Certainly not from Kathleen. Sonny was quiet, but never shy. And nor did it come from Tom, who had often been melancholy in his life, but had always liked the company of others. Truly, it was a trait all of his own, and no effort from the adults around him could ever undo it.

Tom stopped trying. He recognised the futility of it. And the cruelty. Instead, from then on, he valued even more the fact that Jack could be otherwise with him, that the boy would chatter away in Tom's company, as if that was how he always was. They were more precious, those hours, because of the silence that surrounded them.

Still, he worried about him. As did Kathleen, who saw a fragility in her son that was ill-suited to the life into which he'd been born. The world, she knew, could be cruel to quiet boys, and she felt a certain pain in foreseeing that cruelty.

Of the three of them, only Sonny was unconcerned. He felt some disappointment, it was true, that his son was such a timid thing. But he seemed to believe, more so than his wife or Tom, that it would simply pass, that Jack would ease into himself in the end. A few knocks and he'll get up stronger, Sonny thought. He'll figure himself out.

There were certainly knocks. When the time came for Jack to go to the tiny primary school in Treswick, he had to be dragged, near enough, his fingers prised from the doorframe of the house. For the first week, his mother would take him, leave him at the gate with the other children, then take him back again when he chased up the road after her. When eventually he consented to stay put, he looked defeated. Some of the children in the school he had known all of his life – the sons and daughters of the family's neighbours – but still he seemed to struggle to get along with them. He did not make friends easily.

It broke Kathleen's heart to see her boy bowed down like that, burdened by the effort of being among his peers. She could not think of a way to help him, to make his time easier, and so she would coddle him, keep him close, as if in compensation. The gulf between his home and school life increased.

Some of Jack's classmates, sensing weakness, would taunt him without mercy. More than once in his first year or two at school he came home with a bruise or a black eye. The third time it happened, Sonny went to speak to Lawrence Polson, whose boy was responsible. In the man's house, though, he found himself making excuses, blaming his own son for the bullying. 'He likely brings it on himself,' he said. He didn't repeat those words to Kathleen – he was ashamed of them, in hindsight – but things did ease up at the school after that. At least for a while.

When Jack came home in the afternoons, it was Tom who would keep him occupied until Kathleen's work was done. Tom did less on the croft now than ever before. He had let Sonny take more of the strain. He was enjoying his life, and much of that pleasure came from Jack.

# 6

Ordinarily, Jack maintained a relaxed but still fairly active lifestyle. He walked, he worked in the garden, he *did* things with his days. He was conscious of getting older, naturally, but his age had not thus far imposed any restrictions on his activities.

Others he knew were not so lucky. Vina had arthritis in her knees that made her wince as she moved around the shop. Brian, Jack's old boss from the Post Office, had a hip replacement when he was fifty-nine, and was now on the waiting list for another. Then there was Gordon, Vina's husband, who could barely even leave the house.

Jack wasn't especially old, but he was of an age when things felt more likely to go wrong. You developed a vigilance for it, he thought, that was as much a part of ageing as the problems themselves. Any time he woke with an ache or a pain now he would wonder to himself, is this the one that won't ever go away?

One good thing about turning sixty, though, had been

that the guilt he once felt about taking naps during the day had left him entirely. That guilt had been of his father's making. Sonny: a man who never rested unless forced to, a man for whom busyness itself was as important as anything that might actually be achieved by it. Idleness, he detested. 'Get up oot of that bed!' he used to shout at Jack in the morning. The day began at whatever time Sonny happened to wake; and as a man who suffered sleep-ending nightmares for most of his adult life, some days that could be very early indeed.

Sonny was not an especially harsh or demanding father, except when it came to rest. The greatest failure he could imagine for his son was that Jack might be sleeping when others were not. Jack learned to look alert at all times, lest his father use the back of his hand to wake him up.

Though he had not inherited Sonny's disdain for all forms of rest, Jack had carried with him that sense that daylight was not to be wasted on sleep. Any time he felt drowsy, he would swig an extra coffee or go outside, let the cold air keep him lively. But one day, not long after he entered his seventh decade, he sat down in his chair in the late afternoon and closed his eyes. He'd come in from the garden, and had nothing else that needed to be done. He'd leaned his head back in the chair, stretched his legs out and that was that. He slept soundly for more than an hour, and woke feeling utterly refreshed. It seemed unfair that it had taken him so long to discover this luxury. Now, whenever the urge took him, he would nap happily, either seated in the armchair or, sometimes, lying down on the sofa – until Loretta claimed the sofa as her own.

And that's exactly what he was doing: sitting, mouth agape, dreaming he was the lead guitar player in Garth Brooks's band – Garth Brooks, for goodness' sake! He didn't even like Garth Brooks – when the doorbell rang. It was an early, pre-lunch nap for Jack. He hadn't slept well the night before, so he'd allowed himself to top up a little late-morning. The bell didn't wake him fully first time, but on the second ring he opened his eyes, confused. He'd been trying to play a guitar solo on a song he barely knew, in front of a stadium audience, and when he plucked the string it had made an electronic chiming sound: *ding-dong*.

Then he was awake. And so was the cat, who was staring at Jack as though it were he who was responsible for this interruption.

'I'm comin!' he shouted, when his brain settled enough to understand what was happening. 'Just a second.' He pressed down on the arm rests and grudged himself to his feet.

Almost nobody ever rang the doorbell at Jack's house, which only added to his confusion. Anyone who knew him would have just opened the two front doors and yelled, and almost anyone else would have come into the porch then knocked the inside door. The bell was only ever used by people collecting money for charity, or else young men in dark suits trying to convert him. But he hustled to the porch, just in case, rubbing a hand through his hair as he went, so he might look less dishevelled than he felt.

He opened the door.

Vaila was standing in the same bright red raincoat as she'd been wearing yesterday, though there was no more sign of precipitation now than there had been then.

112

'I've come to see the kitten,' Vaila said. 'Loretta. Like we agreed.'

Jack had forgotten until then his brief conversation with the girl the previous evening, and now that he recalled it he was no less surprised that she had come as she said she would.

'Can I see her?' Vaila asked, when Jack failed to respond. 'Please.'

Jack nodded. 'Sure,' he said. 'She's in the livin room. I'll show you.' He turned back into the house, then had a thought. 'I dunna ken if she'll be friendly,' he said, lowering his voice. 'She was shy when she first arrived, but she seems happier now. Hopefully she'll want to see you, if you're quiet and gentle wi her.'

Vaila, just behind him, whispered, 'Okay.'

And she *was* quiet. Though clearly excited, the girl followed Jack into the living room as coyly as if she were meeting some minor celebrity or royal, by whom she was both awed and a little confused.

The two of them stopped in the doorway, and Jack heard a slight intake of breath from behind him.

'She's *beautiful*,' Vaila said. Which was true, he realised, now that it had been pointed out to him. Loretta *was* beautiful.

The kitten was looking at the two of them, eyes wide, ears up.

'If you go to her slowly, she'll maybe let you stroke her,' Jack said. But he needn't have bothered with the advice. By the time Vaila had crossed the room, creeping on her tiptoes, Loretta was sitting up in eager expectation.

She pressed her face into the girl's little hand, rubbing first one cheek then the other, a thick purr erupting from her throat. Then she slumped on one side and lifted a back leg to expose her belly.

Jack laughed. 'Well, she likes you, that's for sure,' he said.

Vaila didn't reply. She had knelt down in front of the sofa, both hands on the kitten: one scratching its side and stomach, the other stroking its face, head and throat.

Jack watched. He felt a twinge of something – what was it? Not jealousy, surely? He never gave Loretta attention quite like this. He had maintained a certain distance up till now. Sometimes he would reach down and give her a scratch as she ate her breakfast, and sometimes she would jump on his lap in the evening and curl up to sleep. But this – this unabashed pleasure that cat and girl were taking in each other – this was different.

'Do you want somethin to drink?' he asked, after a moment longer. Vaila nodded without looking round, and Jack went to the kitchen. What did children drink, then? Not tea, he thought. Milk? He guessed not. And since he had no juice, that left only water. He poured two glasses and carried them through, set one down behind her on the coffee table.

Vaila thanked him. Jack wondered if she were especially polite for an eight-year-old. He thought perhaps she was, but he didn't know any others with whom he could compare her.

She was looking around the room now, taking it in for the first time, having been focused only on the cat when she arrived.

'Do you have any toys for her?' Vaila asked.

'For wha?' Jack replied. 'For Loretta?'

She nodded.

'No. What kind of toys?'

'Well, my friend Abigail makes little mice out of old socks for Fluffy and he loves them. He chases them around, even though he's the one making them move. Loretta might like one.' Her face was very serious.

'Huh,' Jack said. 'I suppose she might. Sometimes she seems to be chasin things aroond when there's nothin there. Imaginin mice, maybe. Or else she chases her tail.'

'A real mouse would be better,' Vaila said. 'A real mouse made of socks, I mean.'

'I'll keep that in mind,' Jack told her. 'I hae a needle and thread here somewhere.'

'I can make one for her.'

'You dunna need to do that.'

She shrugged. 'It's okay. She deserves it.'

Jack had no answer to that.

'Why do you no hae a kitten,' he asked, 'since you like them so much?'

Vaila sat down on the sofa beside Loretta. She stretched her legs out and looked at her feet.

'Mummy won't let me,' she said. 'Not yet. She said I'm not' – she paused for a second to line the word up in her mouth – 'responsible enough to look after it myself.' She stopped again. 'Mummy said I can have one next year. I just have to wait.'

This was exactly what Sarah, her mother, had told Jack in the shop. He liked that it had been explained to Vaila truthfully. It seemed fair.

'A year'll pass quickly,' he said.

The girl looked at him as if he were mad, then seemed to realise what her face was doing. 'Can I be friends with Loretta until then?' she asked.

'Sure,' Jack said, shrugging. 'I think she'd like that.'

Vaila turned back to the cushion beside her, and the kitten squirmed on its side, begging again for attention.

Jack was sitting in the armchair with his guitar in his lap. He wasn't really playing, he was just plucking strings, moving his left hand absentmindedly over the fretboard. His fingers formed the shapes of chords as if that's what they'd been created for, as if these shapes were a knowledge he carried in his bones. But that was a long way from the truth. Jack's ability with this instrument, such as it was, had been hard-earned. He had gathered it against the odds.

The very first guitar Jack owned was a dreadful thing. His parents bought it when he was twelve, and he could still remember the excitement he'd felt when he saw the instrument for the first time. There were vouchers involved, he assumed, some mail-order offer that must have seemed, to them, a bargain. They would have thought that new was preferable to second-hand. But in this case they were wrong.

The guitar looked okay. It had curves in the correct places, and was adorned with the appropriate number of strings. It was an acoustic guitar, which was what he had wanted, and the strings were steel, not nylon, which again was good. But it didn't take too close an inspection to see that this instrument had not been made with care.

Upon arrival in Shetland, one edge was already split; the back was beginning to part from the side. This split would grow in length and width over the coming months, until Jack could look down as he played and see right inside the body of the guitar. Playing, too, was a problem, because while the strings appeared to be connected in the right way, they sat far too high above the fretboard, making the effort of pressing them down inordinately painful. More than once, the highest E-string sliced into Jack's fingertip as he tried to shape a chord.

That he persisted was remarkable, and had he known from the start that his guitar was in fact an impediment to learning, he might well have given up. There was no chance that his parents would replace it, after all. They had neither the money nor the inclination for that. Only the hope of improvement, the dream of making music by himself, kept Jack going. The sounds he wanted to create were what he held always in mind. Those imagined sounds made the pain and the frustration bearable. But only just.

The solution – the salvation, really – came in the unlikely form of Henry, Vina's father. He and Sonny had grown up together, and gone to the whaling together too. He had been best man at Jack's parents' wedding. Where Sonny was serious and short on words, Henry was gregarious and garrulous. As friends, they were a somewhat unlikely pair – near opposites in temperament – but unlikeliness never stopped them. Henry would appear at Hamar at least one evening a week, or else on a Saturday afternoon, with a bagful of beers, most of which he would drink himself. Jack, who found Henry both entertaining and exhausting at once, would often retreat to his room at such times. But not always.

Settling in one night, his third can of export opened, Henry spied Jack's guitar leaning against the wall by the window.

'Let's hae a shot of that,' he said, putting his can down on the carpet, then cracking his fingers outward, like a pianist. 'It's been a while since I played, right enough, but I reckon I can mind what's what.'

Sonny laughed. 'You canna be ony worse as him,' he said, nodding at Jack. Sonny could be cruel in company.

'Hush,' Kathleen said. 'He's just learnin.' She stood and passed the guitar to Henry.

'Yes, yes, give him a chance,' Henry said. 'Takes a lot of practice to soond this good.' He grinned, then stretched his left hand up the neck. His fingers wiggled a bit and took shape; his right hand strummed the strings. A simple G chord, then a C, then another G, more awkward this time. Henry tried something further up the neck: a chord Jack couldn't identify from where he was sitting. The strings buzzed, then muted, as Henry pulled his fingers away.

'Bloody hell!' he said, flapping his left hand in the air, as though it were scalded. 'Where did you get this thing?' He held the guitar up in front of him, saw the crack in the side and prodded it with one finger. He tried to play one more time, then quit. He shook his head and looked at Jack, who was sitting quietly on the stool by the kitchen. 'This,' Henry said, holding it up in one hand. 'This is no a guitar. This is . . . an instrument of torture.'

Sonny laughed, awkwardly, then stopped laughing as Henry stood and left the room with the guitar still in his hand.

The porch door opened and closed, and the three of them went together to the window: Sonny, Kathleen and Jack. They stood watching, appalled, as Henry stopped just outside, lifted the guitar high above his head, then swung it like an axe towards the ground. The body struck the edge of the dry stone garden wall, and in a fraction of a second had ceased to be a body at all. It splintered, seemed almost to explode. Shards of varnished wood sprayed all around.

Henry tossed the neck aside, with its tangle of strings dangling from one end. He brushed a hand down the front of his jumper, to rid himself of the shrapnel, then walked to his car as though nothing had happened. Henry could be unpredictable when he'd had a drink. He could act daft. But this was extreme, even for him.

Sonny clutched for words. 'I'm sorry,' he said to Jack, putting a hand on the boy's shoulder. 'He must be . . . I think he must . . .' Then, at once, he was furious. 'Bastard!' he yelled through the window at the departing car. He turned as if to give chase, but Kathleen stopped him.

'Not now,' she said, worried perhaps that her husband might resort to violence. 'We'll speak to him tomorrow, get this sorted oot.'

Jack felt helpless, close to heartbroken. He was still looking out of the window. 'Shall I go and pick it up?' he asked.

'No,' his father said. 'That's no your job.'

Jack went to his room. He was worried that if he looked at the remains of his guitar any longer he might cry. He shut the door and lay on his bed, staring at the ceiling. He could hear his parents speaking in the living room, their whispers loud enough to carry, but not to be deciphered.

It was hard to tell how much time passed before the sound of tyres on the track reached Jack's room. He was so bereft it felt like hours, but since Henry lived only a few miles down the road, it might just have been fifteen minutes. Jack didn't move. He didn't want to see anyone else that night, and when he heard Henry's raised voice again, he was even more determined to stay put.

A few moments passed. Henry and his father were talking, then his mother too. Sonny sounded angry for a moment, then his voice softened. How easily he forgave his friend, Jack thought.

Then there was a knock on his door.

He didn't answer.

Another knock.

'I'm sleepin,' he said.

'Could you come oot here, please?' his mother replied, in her gentlest voice. 'Henry has somethin he wants to say.'

'Tell him I dunna want to hear it.'

There was a pause, a whispered consultation, then the door opened. Sonny stood there with Kathleen at his side. 'Come oot,' he said. There was no choice this time.

Henry was at the front door, kneeling beside a guitar case. The case was open, and he turned to Jack as he lifted the contents out.

'I'm sorry I smashed your instrument, Jackie,' he said. 'But it was nae use.' He looked at the fingers of his left hand and shook his head. 'It was worse as nae use, in fact. It was bloody awful.'

Henry held the intact guitar out in front of him, turning it face-up. 'This een is mine,' he said. 'It's no new and it's no fancy, but it's ten times better as that shite oot in the garden.' He looked at Kathleen and nodded. 'Which I will tidy up in just a minute.'

'I dunna play it ony more,' he went on. 'And I'm no likely to start again ony time soon, either. So, if you can keep at it, you can keep it. If you give up, you can give it back.'

He gave a strange half-bow as he handed the guitar to Jack, who held it as if it were a precious artefact. And then Henry was gone, into the garden, where the sound of grunting and scraping went on for more than ten minutes, as he picked up every piece that he could find.

Henry was right, the guitar was not fancy. But after months of playing the now-demolished instrument, this one felt as smooth and as comfortable as anything Jack could have wished for. It was bigger too, with a golden finish that even his parents cooed over.

For days, Jack expected Henry to return, sober this time, to say he'd made a terrible mistake, to ask for his instrument back. But it never happened. Henry didn't come back for another fortnight – he was sheepish, still, about his behaviour – and then he only asked how Jack was getting on. The guitar had changed hands, and Jack's playing improved quickly. He spent more time on it than ever, hunched over, watching his fingers until he didn't need to watch them any more, until they knew without direction where they had to go.

Henry's guitar, which he'd bought, he said, in Edinburgh in 1957, on his way home from the whaling, was the only one Jack had until after his parents died. (And he had it still, up in the loft, with those belongings of his mother and father that he couldn't bring himself to throw away.) Then, when the croft was sold, he used some of the money to buy a second-hand Martin: the most perfect instrument he could imagine. The guitar in his hands was the most precious thing he owned.

Vaila returned the next afternoon. Jack was getting home from a long walk – out along the shore for three miles or so, in the direction of Treswick, then back along the road, where he had to dodge a car going far too quickly; he'd almost stumbled into the ditch. He saw the red raincoat from a long way off, and hurried up the track to the house.

'You been here long?' he asked, just a little out of breath.

She nodded, hopping down from the old stone wall on which she'd been sitting. 'It's okay, though,' she said. 'I don't mind.'

'Well, I'm sorry. I didna ken what time you were comin.' He opened the garden gate, which Vaila herself must have closed, since he never did.

She grinned then, remembering something. 'I brought you a present,' she said. 'It's for Loretta.' She fished in her raincoat pocket and pulled out a purple fabric mouse. She held it by the tail – three inches of white string with a knot at the end – and let it dangle. 'I think she'll like it.'

'Did you make that?'

She nodded again. 'Last night,' she said. 'Mummy helped me.'

'Well, that's very kind of you,' said Jack, touched. 'I think she'll like it, too. Let's see, shall we?'

Jack went ahead and opened the front door, hung his jacket on a hook in the porch, then opened the inside door to the hallway. Loretta, who must have been lying in wait on the other side, came bounding past him out into the front garden, almost colliding with Vaila on the way. Once there, she stopped and turned around, as though surprised her escape plan had succeeded.

Jack, who was still nervous about letting her outside, made as if to give chase, but Vaila only laughed. She tossed the little mouse in the air, and when it landed on a flagstone, just a metre or so from Loretta, the kitten understood. She sidled up to the toy, batting it gently at first, and when the fabric caught on her claws and the mouse lifted, momentarily, from the ground, she was transformed. Down she went, into a crouch, then she pounced, grabbing the cloth animal and clutching it between her paws. She rolled over, biting at it and kicking wildly with her back feet, then tossed it to one side, leaping again, as though the mouse had moved of its own volition.

Vaila, watching, was delighted. Jack was just relieved. 'I'm going to get myself some tea,' he said. 'You twa can play oot here. And just come inside if you want.'

He boiled the kettle, squeezed then tossed the tea bag, and sat down. The walk had been a good one: a loop he took every couple of weeks or so if the weather was fine. Today it had been warm enough to take his jacket off for part of the time, and he'd sat for a while by the water, looking out. The seat of his trousers was still a little damp.

Coming back again – always the worst part of a walk – he'd been thinking about a song he was trying to finish, honing the tune, trying out lines in his head. It was funny, he thought, how sometimes they came together quickly, words and music, as though he were remembering rather than than writing them, while other times they resisted taking shape. One line would close the door to another; one word would force a re-evaluation of everything that had come before. With some songs he let himself take short cuts; a half-baked phrase or two was fine. Other times, and for reasons he couldn't fathom, the stakes seemed much higher. Despite the fact that no one was likely ever to hear the song, it really seemed to matter that he get it right.

Jack began writing almost as soon as he began playing guitar. Making those first awkward shapes on the fretboard, spidering his fingers in all directions, it was always just a means to an end. He wanted to play the songs he loved, and he did. He learned them, played along to the records as best he could. But he also wanted to reach beyond that, to make songs of his own. It seemed to him then, as a boy in his early teens, and it seemed to him now, as a man of sixty-two, that there was something outlandish and incred-ible about writing a song: a thing that lived and breathed in the world, that could be animated at will by anyone who chose to do so. A song seemed then a magical thing, and nothing in these past decades had persuaded Jack that this was not the case.

To write one was to create something new in the world, but it was also to step outside that world, beyond the one in which he lived. In a song, Jack could be someone else. Even in the songs born from his own experience – which were few and far between – he was someone else, a character, a host of characters, a panoply of them. He became many people when he wrote and sang. He became bigger than himself, and his life became bigger than the one that he had lived. The bare facts of Jack could say nothing of the many people he had been, the great things he had done, the great loves he had lost and found and lost again. Jack's life had been enormous.

Tea drunk, he went to the living room, stood in front of the wall of music and ran his eyes in patterns across the spines. He wanted something in particular, but he wasn't sure what it was. He would know when his eyes landed upon it. The right sound, right mood.

Not that.

Nor that.

Nor that.

Perhaps? No. Not that.

And then, yes, there it was. George Jones: *that* was what he wanted. Bright and majestic as liquid metal, George Jones was the correct answer to a lot of questions, and this was one of them.

Jack pulled down a CD, a compilation he'd bought, years back, for the single song it held that he didn't already own. He opened the drawer on the stereo and set the disc inside. He sat on the sofa to listen.

He could still remember the first time he'd heard George Jones sing. Not at home – his parents hadn't owned any of his music – but at a friend's house, when he was thirteen or fourteen years old. The sleeve was what drew him in. It looked like a poster for a Hollywood film, gauzy and soft-focused, with George up front, stone-faced, and Tammy

Wynette just behind him, big-haired and glamorous. The record belonged to his friend's mother, and he asked if he could borrow it.

They were a long way from being in vogue back then with boys of his age, but Jack loved the way the two voices seemed so entwined. And he loved as well that blurry line between their real marriage – by then, just about shattered – and the longing and hurt they expressed in song. It wasn't just the cover that seemed like Hollywood.

When he first started learning to sing, Jack had longed for a voice like George's. The sweet, mellifluous twang of it. But dreams like that one die young, punctured, as they must be, by reality. Jack's voice was okay. It did the job. But he was not George Jones.

The CD was five songs in when a door opened, and Loretta came galloping past, to the kitchen. Jack could hear the crunch and gobble of cat biscuits being eaten. Vaila appeared a few seconds later, the mouse dangling, bedraggled, from her hand.

'She liked it, then,' Jack said, lowering the volume on the remote control.

Vaila nodded. 'She likes to play,' she said. 'She's fun.'

'I'm pleased to hear it,' Jack told her.

Vaila looked around the room, then moved towards the stereo. She picked up the CD from the top of the speaker. 'Mummy has some of these as well,' she said. Then, looking up at the wall: 'But not as many as you.'

She held the album in front of her and read the cover to herself. Jack could see her lips move, though she didn't make a sound.

'He's funny-looking,' she said, turning to Jack again. He reached for the case, and agreed. George did look quite funny, with his big forehead and his Lego-man hair.

'I read somewhere,' Jack said, 'that he used to hae his hair cut every single day.' He tried to remember if that was correct. 'His lawn, too, I think.'

'Why would he do that?' Vaila asked. She looked appalled.

'I dunna ken, really,' Jack replied. 'Maybe he was scared of it getting oot of control. You canna control everything, but you can control your hair.'

'That's silly.'

'I suppose so. But folk do silly things sometimes.'

Another song began. 'A Good Year For The Roses': in Jack's opinion, one of the most perfect songs ever recorded.

'Can you turn it off, please?' Vaila asked, after only a few bars.

'Just the song, or all of it?'

'All of it. I don't like it.'

Vaila was honest, as well as polite.

'Sure,' Jack said, and pressed the Stop button on the stereo.

Vaila went to sit on the sofa, where Loretta was licking herself clean, perched on her cushion.

'Does your mam ken you're here?' Jack asked then, a sudden uncertainty in his stomach. The girl had been at the house for a long time.

'I told her I was coming,' she said.

'And she didna mind?'

Vaila shook her head. 'No,' she told him, without looking up. 'Mummy says you're harmless.' She ran a hand down the kitten's back and along the length of its tail.

Jack turned the word over a few times in his head, then repeated it out loud. 'Harmless,' he said. 'Huh.' Then he started to laugh. A big, full-bellied laugh.

Vaila turned to him, confused. 'What's so funny?' she asked.

Jack could not explain it. But nor could he stop himself from laughing.

# Home

Capo 5th? F?

I would steal, I would beg, I would borrow
I would stand in the darkness (all) alone
I would trade all my days for one tomorrow
If it meant I could just be back at home

C/ Home: where the heart is tethered
Home ~~where every road must end~~ stories never
where you go to make amends
Home is where ~~your~~ the stories last forever
Oh I wish that I was back home again.

There's ~~just~~ only one place that I belong to
No matter where I lay my head
~~I know~~ It's where all my ~~dreams~~ hopes have gone to
~~But I don't dream much~~ ~~when all is done & said~~
And where all my ~~hopes~~ dreams have led

C Home...

Now I've been gone for such a long time
(At least) ~~That's~~ how it feels, to me
But now I'm ready to make this ~~moment~~ journey mine
And I know where ~~(it is)~~ I need to be

C Home...

129

# the light bursts in

## 1969

The first thing that happened in 1969 – or not the first thing, but the first thing that anyone at Hamar would remember happening when they thought back to that year – was that Tom died.

The first sign of it was in mid-January. If Tom had felt it coming before then, felt it growing inside him, he did not say so. If he had experienced discomfort previously, he had hidden it well. One evening, over dinner, Kathleen noticed he looked thin, almost frail, and when she mentioned it to him, Tom agreed that he was tired. 'Gettin auld is all it is,' he said. But Tom was not especially old. He was seventy-two, that was all.

Kathleen was not reassured. She kept an eye on him, and it was clear when she started looking that something wasn't right. He was eating less than he used to, and he sometimes touched a hand to his middle, as if a stomach ache might be the problem. He turned a pale grey, and his energy diminished. By the time it really struck him, in the middle of March, it was almost over.

The doctor wasn't certain of the cause, but he didn't look hopeful. Pancreas: that was his educated guess. But Tom would not go with him to the hospital. He didn't need tests or confirmation. He seemed to know, by then, that his luck was up. Something for the pain was all he wanted. Three more weeks and he was gone.

Tom's death set the house at Hamar in shadows. Each of them – Sonny, Kathleen and Jack – was bereft, but of them all, the boy seemed hardest hit. He had known death before, from a distance; his paternal grandfather had died when Jack was six years old. But this was different. Tom was more than just a person. Tom was something solid, like a field or a hill. He had seemed as permanent as the ocean. For days after, Jack looked for him. He seemed unwilling to believe that such a thing as Tom could truly be gone, that he would not, like the spring or the sunlight, return.

Kathleen herself felt much the same way. Tom had once been her grand-uncle, but he had become much more than that. For a decade, he had been entwined in her daily life, in her thoughts. He had been a source of calm, most often, and of good sense. She had depended on him in a multitude of ways. He had made her life better, easier. He had helped to bring up her son. Now that he was gone, it was as if she were newly alone, abandoned into her own marriage.

Sonny, as so often, was less clear about his feelings. All animosity he once had held was now long gone. Tom, more recently, had been like a father to him – especially since his own father had died. It was grief he felt, of course, but it came to him as a dark confusion, a seething, like

131

something putrid trying to get out. He stomped around the croft in those first days afterwards, as though he could out-walk the hurt, or shake it off with hard work. When the tears came, finally, he was in the gloom of the stone shed, with Tom's woodworking tools in front of him on the bench, sharp and immaculate.

The second thing that happened in 1969 was that the lights came on.

There had been lights before, of course. There were Tilley lamps, glowing gold and stinking of paraffin; there were bulbs run off a wet battery that stood in a corner of the kitchen; and for the past five years there had been inter-mittent power from a Lucas wind turbine that Tom had bought off a man in Treswick, when mains electricity there had made it redundant. The turbine was a great thing when it worked, but it was Tom's skill and know-how that had kept it going. Every few weeks, it seemed, it would stop turning, or else it turned and nothing happened. Always, Tom was able to make it right again.

And then Tom was gone.

The mains cable had run beside the road at the end of the track since 1963, but Sonny had so far refused to pay the fee to bring it up to the house. They were doing just fine as they were, he said. Better to be independent, and not rely on the Hydro Board. Once they've got you, he said, before trailing off, leaving the warning to dangle vaguely above his family.

But when the turbine ground to a halt, a month after Tom's death, and when Sonny's embittered tinkering failed, for days, to fix it, his mind was changed. The money was found, and the house connected. The future, inside a slim cable, arrived.

And what a glorious thing it was, Kathleen thought, in those first months of instant electricity, to flick a switch and to know for certain (or close to certain) that light would come. Power: that really was the word. That's what it felt like: power. No longer were they at the mercy of the wind, or their own technological ignorance. What they needed came to them without intervention. It came unhindered. It was magnificent. Grinning, she would stand sometimes beside a switch and push it one way then the other. On, off, on, off. She'd look at Jack and shake her head in wonder. The world had truly changed.

Sonny did not let go of his scepticism entirely. Not at first. He valued the family's self-sufficiency, their lack of dependence on anyone but themselves and their neighbours. But Sonny was a stubborn man, not a stupid one. He knew this particular tide could be resisted only for so long. And there was no doubt that, as it rose, they were lifted. All of them. It brought pleasure and ease to Hamar. Soon, it was only the cost that troubled him.

There were other sources of trouble that year, too. One of which was Tom's will. They had known from the beginning, Kathleen and Sonny, that the house and croft would be theirs when Tom died. He had made that clear from the start. But they'd assumed, always, it would be left to both of them, or even, more recently, to Jack himself, in their care – such was Tom's fondness for the boy. But they were wrong. When the will was read, it was Kathleen alone who inherited everything.

The difference this made to the couple, practically, was negligible. Non-existent, in fact. But on Sonny, it had a peculiar effect, one he felt acutely but could not put into words. For ten years he had lived in a house that belonged to Tom. Now it belonged to his wife. He remained a guest. He had extended their home, with his own money and his own sweat, but still his name was not on the deeds. It arrived as hurt, this feeling, but it soured to an aimless and unspoken anger. He had worked so damn hard, and yet on paper, still, he had nothing. It was impossible to say, either for Sonny or his family, exactly what ingredients his bad temper had at this time. What part grief? What part insult? What part festering old bitterness? He seemed, from the outside, almost to smoulder, and his wife and son knew well to give him distance.

For the first time in their lives together, Sonny and Kathleen had to learn to live as a couple. They were married, then, in a way they had never quite been married before. There was no escaping each other, no possibility of dilution. Tom had been a calming presence in the house. In the aftermath of his death, things were not easy.

Their first big argument was over the belongings that Tom had left behind: two large kists that were stored in the corner of the living room. The first contained most of his clothes, together with a few momentos, a photograph of his parents, old letters, identity documents, a watch he never wore. The other, which had been locked, contained clothes that once belonged to his wife and daughter, together with a black leather-bound bible. The contents smelled musty, almost damp. It had not been opened in many years.

'We've no need for all this,' Sonny said, as he reached inside. 'The kists we can keep, but the rest . . .' He shook his head.

Had he given her more time, Kathleen would have agreed. He was right, after all. They had no need for them. But need was not the issue. There was propriety, respect. Tom was hardly in the ground, and here was her husband tossing what he did not want away.

'For heaven's sake,' she said. 'Will you leave his things alone?'

'They're no *his* things ony more,' Sonny said. 'They're *your* things.'

Kathleen heard a hurt in those words that was deeper than she had realised. She turned it right back on him.

'Yes,' she said, 'they're my things, and I'm tellin you they're stayin. For now, they're stayin.'

Sonny looked at his wife with fury in his eyes. He slammed the kist shut, the metal latch rattling like a chain, then he turned and went outside.

Kathleen knelt down in front of the kist, the old boards on the lid worn soft and smooth from handling. She knew that life would require more from her than it had until then. Sonny's storms were easier to calm through concession than they were to weather. She opened the lid, lifted the clothes out, item by item, rubbing each between her forefinger and thumb. They were simple clothes, well made, and the smell of the woman and girl who had once worn them was long lost. She folded them neatly on the floor, with the bible beside them. The kist stood bare; the pale unfinished wood inside seemed almost too bright to be real. Kathleen sat a little longer, with her hands upon that wood, and thought of how much Tom would be missed, how empty the house had become.

# 7

Jack had never learned who it was who'd left Loretta on his doorstep. Her origins remained a mystery. He thought about this sometimes, wondering where she might have come from. But he was wont, now, to think of her arrival not as a practical joke but as a gift. More and more, he was grateful.

Once the kitten had made it clear that she did not wish to flee, that she now considered Hamar to be her rightful home, Jack was content to let her wander. She, in turn, learned quickly how to make her desires known. When she wanted to go out, she would sit by the porch, on her haunches, and cry out, or else scratch at the carpet by the door. When the time came to return, she would hop up to the window ledge of the living room and peer in, bobbing her head like an owl. If she spotted Jack inside, she would make a racket until he saw her. If she didn't, she would try another window.

Though he liked to see her outside enjoying herself, prowling or prancing or pouncing, Jack did wonder if

Loretta might be letting the novelty of this new-found freedom get the better of her judgement. Some days, she would be in and out of the house repeatedly. On one occasion, Jack had only just closed the door to let her out when she appeared at the window begging to come in again. He cursed, then laughed, then returned to the door.

Even outside, Jack discovered, Loretta liked company. In the afternoons, she would sit watching from the bench while he pottered in the garden, or else she would slink between the rows of vegetables, her tail held high, like a periscope, looking for something to chase.

In the morning, when Jack went for his pre-breakfast walk, Loretta would trot along beside him, though rarely straying too far from the house. Once beyond the first fence she seemed unnerved – unnerved by the sheep in the field, unnerved by the lack of places to hide. The first morning, she came with him just a dozen metres or so across the grass, then scampered back alone. The next, she went a dozen more. By the end of the week, she would follow all the way to the bottom of the steep ridge, where the grass became scrubbier and thick wedges of granite protruded. There she would pause, look one way then the other, as if the slope were an impenetrable border. As Jack took the path upwards, she would look perturbed a moment longer, mew, then turn and make her way to the fence line, just to the south, returning across the field as close to the wire as she was able, alert to imagined dangers.

By the time Jack got back from his walk, Loretta would be sitting on the window ledge, or else by the porch door, with a look on her face that Jack read either as hurt or else an intense feline disgruntlement.

'Come on, then,' Jack would say. 'Let's hae some breakfast.'

The girl, Vaila, didn't come back every day. 'Mummy said I shouldn't bother you so much,' she told him, one afternoon. But she was no bother, really.

If Loretta was outside when Vaila came up the track, the girl wouldn't interact with Jack at all. He'd only know she was there when a squeal of delight gave her away, or else he'd hear her cooing over the kitten just outside the window.

If Loretta was inside, Vaila would knock gently then come in – as Jack had instructed her to do – seeking out the kitten and spending ten or fifteen minutes alone with her, before heading home again. Loretta seemed to enjoy these visits, and so did Jack. He bought fruit juice from the shop, so he had something more to offer her than water. He bought some biscuits, too.

Before she left, Vaila would usually share a few words with him. She would tell him something about her day, about one of her friends from school, or else she would express some opinion about the cat with which he couldn't help but agree. 'Her white paw makes her very special,' Vaila told him one day. And she was right, of course. It did.

When she was not outside, much of Loretta's time was consumed by sleeping. Sleeping was truly what she was best at. She had, by now, expanded greatly her range of snoozing places. She could be found on the back of the sofa, stretched out like a fox stole, her chin resting on her extended front legs. She could be found inside the box in which she had arrived, stored now in the back bedroom.

She could be found on the sheepskin rug in front of the fireplace, where she would knead her claws into the matted wool, then roll onto her back in unconscious ecstasy. She could be found curled up like a furry whirlpool at the dead centre of Jack's bed. She could be found on Jack's lap as he listened to music. There she'd curl up, head on paws, and purr so loudly he had to turn up the volume on the stereo. If, as he usually did, Jack began to tap his hand on his leg in time to a song, Loretta would open one eye and look up at him, as if to say, *Can't you see I'm trying to rest? Can't a cat get some peace in her own home?* And he would stop, and she'd return to her snoring.

She could be found almost anywhere and everywhere else in the house at one time or another, including, once, in the washing machine, after he'd thrown a towel inside to be cleaned. When he came back an hour later with the rest of the load, she appeared at the machine door, yawning, like a dragon at the mouth of a cave. Jack had yelled in shock, then felt a deep panic at what might have happened had he not seen she was in there.

Loretta, asleep and awake, was by now the source of a great deal of the pleasure and amusement Jack found each day. He had almost forgotten what it was like to live without her.

The bell above the shop door tinkled, and Vina emerged, like a slow motion jack-in-the-box, from below the checkout. Jack gave her a look.

'I was just tyin my shoelaces,' Vina said. 'It takes me a moment to get vertical again.'

For as long as Jack could recall, Vina had worn those rubbery slipper things around the shop. The ones with all the holes in them.

'I fancied a change,' she said, when he mentioned this. 'Now I'm regrettin it.'

'There's a lesson there,' Jack told her.

'A lesson aboot footwear or aboot change?' Vina asked.

'I've nae idea,' Jack said. 'Probably neither.'

'You're a wise man, Jackie.'

Jack grinned, shrugged, and reached for a basket. He headed first for the fridges.

'So I hear you've made a new friend, then,' Vina called out, as he reached in for a carton of milk. He checked the date on it, then swapped the carton for another.

'Wha's that, then?' he asked, without looking up.

'Vaila,' Vina replied. 'Her mam was in here this week, said she and you are great pals these days.'

Jack turned to the freezer. He needed some peas and frozen carrots. 'I dunna think so,' he said. 'She hardly kens I'm there half the time. She's friends wi the cat.' Jack did not use Loretta's name in front of anyone other than Vaila.

'That's no what Sarah telt me,' Vina went on. 'She said the lass comes hame wi all kinds of news: aboot the garden, aboot the hoose. You even *sang* for her, I heard. That's no somethin many folk can say.'

Jack had not, in fact, sung for Vaila. The girl had merely walked into the house one afternoon while he was singing, and he hadn't heard her arrive. She'd stood behind his chair until the song was finished, then almost gave him a heart attack by clapping. Jack's cheeks had scorched red with embarrassment.

'Well,' Vina said, 'I'm glad you're bein nice to the lass. She's had a hard time of it wi her dad leavin. It's probably good for her to spend time wi someen that's no her mam.'

There was a lot to think about in what Vina had just said, and Jack didn't reply for a moment as he considered it. He felt a peculiar pang at the thought of Vaila sad. He didn't like to imagine her upset.

'She's a fine lass,' was what he said.

Vina nodded, and they left it at that.

From the shop, with two bags bulging on the passenger seat beside him, Jack decided to stop en route. He turned the corner onto his track, then pulled over, just in front of Sarah's fence. He wasn't a hundred per cent sure what he was going to say to her, but the conversation at the shop had made him realise that he ought to have talked to her before. He ought to have asked if it was okay for Vaila to be in the house. He ought not to have taken the girl's word for it.

He shut the car door and went up the steps, closing the gate behind him. He knocked, waited, then knocked again.

He was just about to turn around and go when Sarah appeared, dressed in overalls and covered in paint. 'Sorry,' she said, out of breath. 'I was upstairs, redecorating the spare room. It took me a moment to get off the step-ladder without making a mess.' She laughed. 'Sorry to keep you waiting.'

'That's okay,' Jack said. 'It's a fine colour.' He pointed at the blue-green streak on her left hand.

She smiled. 'It is, yes. Very . . . calming? Maybe? To be honest, I just wanted a change. It's been plain white since we moved in. I was desperate to change something, and that was the easiest room to mess around with.'

Jack nodded, slowly. He was trying to find the right way to begin, but he wasn't sure exactly what needed to be said. Sarah saved him.

'I've been meaning to come and see you, actually,' she said, stepping aside from the door. 'Come in, come in.' She was gone before Jack could resist, and he followed her, leaving his boots outside on the porch.

The wide hallway was lined with photographs, most of them of Vaila when she was younger, with a few landscapes in between. Some he recognised, some not. Turning to the left, into the enormous open-plan kitchen and dining room, Jack noticed first the homely clutter, the sense of a space that was lived in. But he was distracted then by the wide windows, which looked out onto the fields beyond the main road. A glimmer of ocean could be seen from here, a slim wedge towards the southeast, and Jack felt sorry that his own view, from Hamar, was more restricted.

'Do you want a cup of something? Tea, coffee, water, juice?' Sarah pointed at a chair on one side of the dining table, indicating that he should sit down. She didn't pause long enough for him to answer her question. 'So, as I said, I'd meant to come and say thank you. And sorry, too. I didn't mean for Vaila to foist herself on you like this. I thought she'd just go and see the cat a couple of times then forget about it. I didn't realise . . .' She gave an apologetic shrug. 'She seems to have become quite attached.'

'She's fond of the kitten, that's for sure,' Jack said.

'She's fond of you, too.'

Jack blushed and mumbled his dissent.

'Was this what you were coming to speak to me about?' Sarah asked. 'I didn't give you a chance to say.'

'It was, yes.'

'Oh, sorry! Look,' she put her hands flat on the table, 'don't worry. I can tell her not to come up again. That's not a problem at all. She's quite an intense little thing, I know, and if you're not used to kids . . .' She winced. 'I don't actually know if you're used to kids or not, Jack, I just sort of assumed . . .'

'It's fine,' Jack said. 'I'm no. But that's no what—'

'I probably ought to relent and let her have a kitten of her own,' Sarah went on. 'I'm just being stubborn about it, to be honest. Once I said no, I felt I had to stick to it. But she's so keen, I think she'd look after it perfectly well. I just didn't want—'

This time it was Jack who interrupted. 'That's no what I wanted to say,' he told her, before Sarah talked everything out of shape. 'It's no problem her visitin. She's good as gold. And the kitten loves the attention. I just wanted to make sure that you're okay aboot it. We hadna discussed it, and I just thought maybe we should do that.' Jack still wasn't exactly certain *what* they should discuss, but he knew there was something.

'Oh, thank goodness!' Sarah said, putting a hand to her chest. 'I was acting very cool about it there, but I think Vaila would have been devastated if she wasn't allowed to visit.' She laughed. 'She's a sensitive soul, you know.'

'She's a fine lass,' Jack said, for the second time that morning.

'*Thank* you! Yes, she really is. And please, if she gets a bit much, or if she comes around too often, just let me know and I'll tell her to ease off. And don't be afraid to shoo her away sometimes. She'll do what she's told.'

'You dunna mind her comin, then?'

'*Mind* it? God, no! I love my daughter to pieces, but I'm never sorry to get an hour or two to myself. Parenting is a whole lot more . . . *intense* since Gary left, you know.'

Jack nodded. He could imagine that it would be.

'So, I'm very grateful that she's found somewhere she can go by herself. Somebody who doesn't mind her hanging around.'

'Somebody . . . harmless,' Jack said.

Sarah looked at him for a second, then slapped her palms to her cheeks in horror. 'Oh God, did she *say* that to you? Oh no, Jack, I am so sorry. Children are . . . God, I'm so embarrassed.' Her face was sheer scarlet.

Jack let Sarah suffer, briefly, then smiled. 'There's worse things to be as that,' he told her. He chuckled, then she too began to laugh.

'I need to have a *serious* chat with that girl,' Sarah said, 'about what should and should not be shared with other people.'

'She's a fine lass,' Jack said, for the third time.

Sarah stood, still blushing, and asked Jack again if he wanted a drink. This time he nodded. 'Tea would be splendid,' he said.

As she filled the kettle and rummaged in one of the

cupboards for mugs, Jack wondered if perhaps it was she, Sarah, who was lonely. It must be hard for her, he thought. It must be hard.

When he got back up the road to the house, just before lunch, Vaila was in the garden, a long piece of string raised in one hand, with the kitten leaping up to catch the dangling end. Jack watched her for a moment from the car, laughing.

Jack had always been pretty good at keeping up with the various tasks and jobs that kept his house and garden going. His encounter with Sarah reminded him that he hadn't actually painted inside or outside for at least a decade, and it showed. But other than that, when it came to repairs, to maintenance, to basic upkeep, he did okay.

Some of the jobs he enjoyed, or tolerated without much effort, and he would try to keep on top of these, without letting them go too long undone. He knew that a chore ignored would only become bigger as time went on. He didn't have a list to tick things off, even in his head. He just knew, after a lifetime in this house, what would need doing and when.

Of all these tasks – the ones that came around regularly and which could be predicted, as opposed to the occasional emergency fix, for which he sometimes needed assistance – the one he disliked most of all was the annual repair of the track from the main road up to the house.

The track had first been laid by Tom, his mother's grand-uncle, whom Jack remembered still, the presence of him, with an intensity that belied the half-century since his death. Tom had upgraded the track from the pair of muddy ruts that provided access until the 1950s. At one point, in the late seventies, the council had offered to take ownership and pave it properly, but Sonny, proud old mule that he was, had told them where to go. So it remained unsurfaced, loosening and pitting in the winter rains, so that, by spring, Jack's car would bounce its way from the house down to the road.

At some point each summer, without warning or discussion, a truck would arrive and dump a load of hardcore by the shed wall. It was Young Andrew who brought it. The agreement was that Andrew would pay for the material if Jack did the work. It had seemed fair at the time – anything that avoided expenditure on Jack's part seemed fair to him. But as he got older, as the work grew more effortful and time-consuming, he had begun to question the deal, and to wonder if, at some point, it might be renegotiated.

The pile of crushed rock had been lying there for several days now. Several dry days, ideal for this particular task. But on those days Jack had found some other, more appealing way to occupy his time, and so each morning, as he headed out for his walk, he had looked at the pile, sighed, and promised himself he would get to it soon. Another day.

Today was that day.

He had dressed appropriately: overalls, steel toe-capped boots, and even a hat to stop his bald spot from burning. He dragged the wheelbarrow out from the shed, and then, exhausted already by the thought of the work to come, he began. Shovelling hardcore, that was the job: first into the barrow, then into each pothole in turn, overfilling so he could tamp them down with the roller later. (This, too, Andrew had provided.) The further away from the shed he got, the harder the task became.

It was his back that began to ache first, a grumble of pain low down, creeping higher like damp as the day wore on. By mid-afternoon his arms hurt too, and his shoulders, and possibly his neck as well, though by that time the pain was so widespread it was hard to be sure where exactly it was coming from.

He'd got two-thirds of the way down the track by that time. When he was younger, Jack could usually get the whole job finished – filling and rolling – in a single day. Now, always, it took more. He would fill one day and roll the next. This was the first year, though, that he had considered giving up without even getting the first part of it done. He looked at his watch, looked at the remaining unmended track, looked at the empty wheelbarrow, and looked back up to the pile of hardcore at the shed, now much-diminished.

He would take a break.

At this stage, the obvious thing to do would be to walk back to the house, have a glass of water and sit down for a moment, before filling the barrow. But Jack knew that if he did that he was unlikely to get up again. If he wanted to finish this part of the job today – which he really did want to do – then he couldn't go inside until it was done.

Jack sat on the grass verge beside the track, his legs stretched out in front of him, his hat abandoned on the ground. His shirt was stuck to his back with sweat. His forehead was slick.

'Christ,' he said out loud. Then, after several deep breaths, again, 'Christ.'

Jack arranged himself so he could lie back on the grass, with his head against the highest part of the bank. The ground here was out of the reach of hungry sheep, so it grew long and lush, and was surprisingly comfortable, despite the lumps and bumps. He closed his eyes.

Back when his father was living, the two of them would do this job together, once Jack was old enough, each urging the other wordlessly on. If they started first thing, they could get it done by early afternoon. His father had never complained about aches or pains so far as Jack could recall. He had always seemed as strong as granite; as persistent and invulnerable, too. And since Sonny had died a young man, only forty-two, perhaps he never did feel the kind of aches that Jack felt now. Or perhaps, once he got home from the whaling, once his body had experienced that, everything else had felt effortless in comparison.

Jack found it hard to imagine his father as a whaler, though he'd heard stories of that time over and over, though they formed the half-mythical backdrop of his childhood. In truth, he found it hard to conjure a clear image of his father these days, one not constructed from a photograph. His memory now was more essence than detail. A feeling of the man, of his intensity, his silent determination, his dedication to work and family, his fury. And his love, too. Though Sonny never spoke that word aloud, at least not to Jack's recollection, Jack had never doubted that his father loved him, that he wanted, above all, what was best for his wife and his boy. Young though Jack had been, he had always felt aware somehow that his father's anger was only ever a kind of confusion. He would have aged, Jack thought, into a mellower man.

He tried to pull Sonny's face into his mind, but he was struggling to focus. Each time he reached for a particular memory, his thoughts would soften and drift, and he would lose what he was aiming for. His breaths deepened, and he plunged helplessly towards sleep.

His mother was yelling at him. Not angrily, just with a certain urgency. She was calling his name. Then again, louder. But when he tried to reply, his mouth wouldn't work. He looked at her, saw the features of her face melted with age, or else with—

'Jack. Wake up!'

He opened his eyes.

Some time had passed. That was the first thing he noticed, though he couldn't say quite what it was that gave the fact away. The light, perhaps. The sun was not where it had been when he lay down.

The second thing he noticed, when he sat up straight, was Vaila, with a tray in her hands, looking at him with some concern on her face.

'Are you okay?' she asked.

He nodded, not quite ready to speak. His mouth felt dry. He looked at his watch. He'd slept for almost an hour.

'I brought you some biscuits and some tea and juice,' Vaila said. 'Mummy said I should. Do you want it?'

Jack nodded again, still dazed. 'I'd love that,' he said. 'Thank you, and thanks to your mam as well.'

Vaila came closer, and laid the tray down beside him. There was a flask, a bottle of juice, two plastic cups and a packet of digestives. Rarely had anything looked so appetising.

Vaila sat on the grass so the tray was between them.

'I can't open the juice,' she said. 'You'll have to do it.'

'Sure,' Jack said. He wiped his hands on his overalls, set the two cups side by side, opened the bottle and poured.

'How long were you standin there?' he asked.

She shrugged. 'I'm not sure. I said your name five times, but you didn't wake up. Then I said it another time and you did.'

'I thought you were my mother,' Jack said. Vaila glanced at him. 'In my dream, I mean,' he added. 'I was confused.'

'Why were you lying on the ground like that?'

'I was tired, that's all. I've been oot here workin all day, and I'm a bit . . . well, I'm a bit oot of practice. Or a bit auld maybe.'

Vaila sipped her juice, holding the cup with both hands. 'How old are you?' she asked.

'I'm sixty-two.'

'That *is* old.'

'It feels like it some days, yes.' Jack took a drink, then reached for the biscuits. 'How auld are you?' he asked, pulling two digestives out between his fingers, and passing one of them to Vaila.

'Eight years and five months. My birthday is in March. When is yours?'

Jack thought about that. 'It's next month,' he said. 'The eighth.'

'That's soon,' she said.

'It is.'

'Can I come to your birthday party?'

Jack laughed. 'If I was havin a party you could come. Definitely. But I've no had one of those since I was, well, a little bit aulder as you.'

'Oh,' Vaila said. She looked sad, though whether she was sad for him or for her he wasn't sure. 'What are those?' she asked, when her disappointment had passed. She was looking behind Jack, at the tall spires of angelica towering above the ditch.

Jack told her what they were. 'My favourite flower,' he said. 'I like the way they're really lots of flowers pretendin to be just wan.' He grabbed a stem and pulled it towards him to demonstrate, showing how each messy white head was constructed of many smaller heads, which in turn were built of tiny pale florets. Vaila peered at the plant, not questioning his unconventional choice.

'Do you hae a favourite flower?' Jack asked.

She shook her head. 'Mummy does,' she said. 'But I don't know what they're called.'

Jack nodded solemnly.

'What have you been doing here?' Vaila pointed at the wheelbarrow.

'I'm just makin the road smooth, so it doesna hurt my car. I fill up all the holes every summer.'

'Who digs the holes?'

'The rain does.' Jack finished his biscuit and reached for another.

Vaila looked at him, unsure if he was pulling her leg.

'What would happen if you left them?'

152

'I suppose they'd get bigger. Then I'd hae to park at your hoose and walk up the track.'

'Hmm,' Vaila said. 'Well, there is room at our house for an extra car. Daddy took his one away.'

'Thanks,' said Jack. 'But it's likely best if I can drive all the way to mine. It makes life easier in the long run.'

'I guess so.' Vaila shook her head when he offered her another biscuit. 'I'm only allowed one,' she said. Then, 'Can I help you?'

Jack smiled. 'I wish you could,' he said. 'It's kind of you to offer. But I think the wheelbarrow might be a bit heavy for you, at least when it's full.'

'Can I push it when it's empty?'

'You can, yes. You can wheel it back up to my hoose, if you want, and then I'll fill it up again. How does that soond?'

Vaila nodded, her mouth full of the biscuit she was eating despite what her mother had said. She stood up, left the tray and its contents where they were. Jack put the cups back, and poured himself some tea into the lid of the flask. By the time they returned with the hardcore it would be cool enough to drink, he thought.

Vaila was already standing behind the barrow. She lifted the two arms with some difficulty – they were exactly the wrong height for her, or she for them – but eventually she found a way that worked. They set off, the two of them, Jack walking alongside Vaila, as slowly as she needed. They took several breaks en route, when Vaila would rub her hands together and grin as she lifted and set off again, Jack thinking all the time of that tea, still steaming on the green verge behind them.

# LORETTA

Loretta, you're sleeping so soundly sweetly
You won't hear the these words that I say sing
Your ~~breath~~ heart it is beating so
   I'll keep my voice down ~~and~~
   make hardly a sound
cos I don't want to wake you again

Loretta, I used to be lonesome
        times
There's days when I still feel that way
               these
But seeing you sleep so soft & so sweet
             no worries, no cares
I don't feel so lonesome today.

Loretta, it's late in the evening
~~But I don't want this day to end~~ yet
So let ~~you sleep on,~~ ~~~~
I ought to be sleeping now too
      so glad
But I'm ~~happy~~ to be with you beside me
and I don't want this day to be through.

# the collection

With Tom gone, Jack's quietness came home. The awkward boy that others had known before was the boy that his parents knew now as well. His jollity and ease were less evident than ever. He seemed not unhappy exactly but smaller somehow, as though he could take up less space in a world without Tom.

What animated the boy most, what brought him to life in ways that nothing else could, was music. Kathleen and Sonny had stumbled across this fact long before. They had seen how he would stop what he was doing at the sound of the wireless or the record player, how he would move closer to the source of it, unable to concentrate on anything but what he could hear. It was funny at first, to see a six-year-old boy staring at a Lefty Frizzell record as it spun on the turntable, every bit of attention he could muster craning towards that sound.

As he got older, Jack's interest became more active. He wouldn't wait for someone else to put music on, but would pick something himself. There wasn't a lot to choose between in Hamar, back then. Sonny had bought a dozen or so records, years before, and the collection hadn't grown much since then. His initial enthusiasm had waned, overtaken by other preoccupations. Once in a while he or Kathleen would take a notion and pull something from its sleeve, but more often they would just hum the songs to themselves as they worked.

By the time Jack was eleven years old, he knew every song on every record in the house by heart. He had played each one until his parents were sick of them. Sometimes he would turn on the wireless instead, but the music he liked – the music he had discovered on those records – was not so easy to locate on the radio. And so Kathleen asked around, for her own sake as much as her son's, and a few more albums arrived, from neighbours and from friends. The collection was expanding.

Nobody could quite remember, later, when Jack first expressed an interest in playing an instrument. Such was his hunger for music that it seemed an obvious progression, and the question had more or less formed itself before he ever had the chance to ask it. A fiddle, though relatively easy to come by, was not going to cut it, that was clear. Jack wanted to sing. He wanted to play the guitar.

Sonny's interests were evolving, too. He had bought himself a boat, much to the surprise of Kathleen. As it happened, he had wanted one for some time, but had kept this wish entirely to himself. He could not find a way to justify such a purchase in financial or practical terms, it was just a thing that he *wanted*. And so, as if ashamed of his unreasonable desire, he kept quiet about it until the deal had been done.

She wasn't new, this boat, but nor was she very old. One previous owner, now deceased, a man who had taken good care of her, had painted the hull afresh each winter, and had made small repairs before they ever became large ones. She was a very fine boat indeed, Sonny thought, twenty feet long, and as sleek and slick as a seal. He took her to the pier at Treswick and tied her up. Often, he would drive out in the evenings just to look at her, or to sit there and tinker with her, pretending there was work he needed to do.

In those first months after the boat arrived, Sonny some-times found himself dreaming of whales. Fleets of them, pods of them, herds. And who could be surprised? He had renamed the boat, from the *Mary Moore* to the *Wayfarer*, after the last ship he'd sailed on in the Antarctic, so his mind was often back in those times. He would think about his months in the far south neither with nostalgia nor regret, but with curiosity, as if the young man – the boy, really – he looked back on were someone else, someone other than himself. He was both sustained and at times horrified by what that boy had witnessed. The whales he dreamed of, though, were not hunted or dismembered. They were, like those he had sometimes seen in the years since he returned from South Georgia, peaceful and content. They seemed like good company to him.

Kathleen, back then, felt uncomfortably adrift. Her husband and her son had become stranger to her than ever before. A distance had opened up between each of them, and she did not know how to cross it. She turned – as Sonny always had – to her work for company. She spent more hours in front of the knitting machine, sometimes feeling needles of pain from her lower back up to her shoulders. And she would visit, too, as Tom used to do, going to see her sister or her friend Leanne in Treswick. She was a sociable woman, living with two near-silent men. There were days when neither her husband nor her son would speak more than a word to her, and she longed not just for company, but for something into which she could escape, something to care about, as Sonny and Jack had found.

The house, then, was a quiet place. Quiet, except for the sound of Jack strumming at his guitar, the strings buzzing and clunking beneath his soft, slow fingers. Kathleen admired the persistence with which her son had set about the task of learning. She could hardly believe, sometimes, that it was her little boy cradling that instrument, his lower lip clenched between his teeth, his eyes fixed on the fretboard. There were times, in fact, though she never told anyone this, that she sat on the floorboards outside his bedroom, listening to the chords forming, to the notes straining into place. And though she could not have explained exactly why it made her cry, that half-formed sound, that's what happened. She listened, feeling the tears creep down her cheeks, not thinking of anything in particular, just hearing that cumbersome music, with a closed door between herself and her son.

# 8

The main thing about country music, the key feature, thought Jack, in an internal monologue that took the form of a lecture – a habit to which he, and perhaps other solitary people (how would he know?), was prone – was restlessness. It was a longing for elsewheres and elsewhens, for places and people and times that were not here, now. It was trepidation, too, about what might be, and regret about what was. It was the desire for things to be otherwise, and the unshakable feeling that, if things were good right now, it couldn't last; trouble was surely on the way. It was a kind of instability, in other words, a present that was constantly undermined, by yearning, by nostalgia, by remorse. It was the existence of alternative lives: better, simpler lives, usually – in the past, present or future – towards which a singer gazed, as if towards a heavenly island shimmering on the horizon.

Jack paused. His confidence in this idea had expanded as it progressed, and he wondered if he ought to be writing it down. He leaned forward to find his notebook, then stopped, leaned back. Why bother? Who would care? There was no one he could tell this kind of thing to, no one who'd be interested in what he had to say, no one in front of whom he could even admit to such notions. His confidence shrivelled again. There was nothing new in all of this, anyway. Every one of his thoughts had been thought before, a thousand times. And maybe, ultimately, *all* songs were about the same feelings, the same few basic urges. In a culture where emotional discourse was discouraged, songs were an acceptable way to express unspeakable longings. Jack figured that country came from such a place. As did he.

It wasn't just the content of country songs that was restless, though; it was the *sound,* too. This was a music – a form, a genre – wholly shaped by movement. Think of Hank Williams: the slither and moan of the fiddle and steel guitar. Think of Jimmie Rodgers: that rollocking brakeman's yodel. Think of the finger slide on a double bass, the quicksilver twang of a Telecaster – and the twang of the human voice, too, the wrung-out, worn-down, kinked and twisted vowels. Think of the pedal steel, for heaven's sake! No instrument is more defined by motion, by the keening of one note towards another. And no sound is more unmistakably country. This music was immune to stillness.

Jack had lived almost his entire life in one place. Other than the few weeks he spent in Glasgow, more than four decades ago now, and the handful of holidays he'd taken over the years, he had been here, in this house, enclosed by these fields, overlooked by this ridge of rock, since he was born. This was a fact he looked on quite differently at different times, like a feature of the landscape altered by the changing light.

Most mornings, as he set off up the hill on his walk — these days with Loretta alongside him — he simply could not imagine being anywhere else. He knew this place as well as he knew himself, and these two pieces of knowledge were not separable but part of the same understanding. He belonged to Hamar. And though on paper the land was no longer his, though it was owned by his neighbour, it still — in some fundamental, bone-deep way — belonged to him.

On these mornings, these days, Jack felt nothing close to restlessness, at least in that geographical sense. The longings he experienced were not directed towards the horizon. He was, in this particular way, a contented man, and he understood this to be a blessing. This was where he was born and where he would die, and he was all right with that.

But regret, he felt. And nostalgia, too. And he felt, as well, a kind of backward yearning for which he did not have an adequate word. He wished sometimes, with an intensity that could knock him almost off his feet, that he had lived a different life, that he had not returned to Shetland to live, that he had been bolder, that he had more urgently pursued the naïve dreams he once had entertained, that he had crashed headlong into their impossibility rather than simply abandoning them — abandoning himself — to what had once felt like fate.

When his parents died, Jack came home because he had to; there were things that needed to be done, practicalities to which he had to attend. But he stayed because he couldn't bring himself to set out towards uncertainty again. He had nowhere in particular to go, and so he didn't. It was an agonising inertia that put an end to the life he had once almost imagined.

Jack had wanted to be a singer, that was the truth of it. He had never admitted that out loud, not to a single person. But it was the only thing that he had ever, with such intensity, desired. Or near enough the only thing.

He did not believe that if his parents had lived this wish would have been fulfilled. Not even for a moment. He was not daft. He was a man of middling talent, brought up on an island in the North Atlantic, many thousands of miles from the home of the music he loved. He had been born entirely in the wrong place, without the confidence or the zeal or the ability to overcome that impediment.

Jack Paton had wanted to be a country singer, a man whose words and voice could ease broken hearts, whose songs could lift and carry listeners back to themselves. He had wanted to stand on a stage, to fill a room with his music, and to see people moved, to see them smile and weep, to know they would leave that room with his melodies between their lips, his lyrics smouldering in their thoughts.

He had wanted all of that, and he had allowed himself, for the briefest of moments, to imagine it. He had gone – in a moment of desperate impulse, he had gone – allowing this spark of desire to carry him. But he came home. He let himself let go.

For forty years, the songs he had written held fragments of the life that Jack had not lived. When he wrote them, he leaned towards that other life, towards the man he had not been. There was richness in that proximity, for which he felt himself lucky, and there was pain, too. He knew no ache as deep as the one that lay between himself and that other, long-lost Jack.

For many months after he returned from Glasgow, his parents missing, presumed drowned, Jack experienced a suffering for which, back then, he had no name. No good words. People were kind to him. His neighbours, his parents' friends. They looked out for him, invited him for meals, helped him with the croft. They tried to keep him on his feet. Jack was conscious of their kindness, but it glanced off him, like light bouncing off a blade. He felt impervious, then. Or, more accurately, he did not feel. He woke, he worked, he ate, he slept. That was all. He passed through his days, a creature only semi-sentient. He was alive, but he was not living.

The croft suffered. That autumn, Jack sold his father's lambs – *his* lambs then – and put down some of the older ewes. He did not replace them. Nor did he let the ram out to do its work as winter approached, but instead left it in its little park alone. The ram, overcome with frustration, leapt two fences and knocked down a third to get to where it wanted to go. Old Andrew, with considerable difficulty, took the animal away.

Jobs piled up. Repairs went undone. The shed was damaged in a storm; a sheet of corrugated tin roof landed halfway down the drive, and for several weeks the hole remained uncovered. Sheep, limping, went untended to.

Some days, Jack's body seemed to weigh more than he could lift. Each movement took more effort than he could muster. He could find no comfort. He was at home, and yet he was as far as it was possible to be from everything that word was meant to mean. It was as though he were floating, held up only by the air inside of him.

He was lost. Hopeless. Stricken.

Jack decided early on not to keep the croft. The work required of him a care he couldn't then find in himself. He performed it grudgingly, doing only the bare minimum. The animals deserved better. The land deserved better.

When he first raised the possibility of selling, Old Andrew winced and shook his head. 'You'll regret it,' he said, looking back across the road, towards his own fields. 'You'll think differently in a year or twa. It'll all come back to you.'

Andrew had seen how hard Jack's father had worked on that croft, how much of Sonny's time, his effort, had been expended on the place. Andrew was the kind of man for whom such effort mattered. It had meaning. To see Jack fritter it away, sell it as though it were a mere possession, it offended him. Jack could see that. But he could see, too, Andrew's sympathy, his sorrow. He saw that sorrow everywhere. Sonny had not always been the most agreeable of men, but his death, Kathleen's death, it had hurt people. It was a wrong that couldn't be righted. It was a wound in the community. People looked at Jack and they felt pain in themselves. He could not escape it, that pain. He felt, at times, like the source of it.

Andrew agreed to buy the land himself, though he made Jack wait a full year. He didn't need it, didn't even want it really, but he didn't want anyone else to have it either. He offered every escape route he could think of, promised to sell it back at the same price at any time in the future. But Jack never did regret his decision. The sale, though it came with some guilt when he thought of his father, and of Tom, brought mostly relief. It took from him a burden that he was unable to carry. Once it was gone, he had no desire to lift it again. He felt a need − and that was the right word, *need* − to live without responsibility for anything or anyone but himself.

That feeling had never really gone away. Jack had lived his life accountable to no one but himself, and to his various employers, none of whom had ever asked of him more than he was able to give. It had been a life of freedom, there was no doubt about that. Jack's ties were minimal, his obligations few. It had been necessary, this freedom, to survive, to climb out of the hole his parents' deaths had dug for him. And he was grateful to Andrew, always, for allowing it.

But freedom . . . well, Kris Kristofferson was right about that.

Jack had lost everything back then, near enough. He had walked away with just enough to live.

One morning, warmer than the previous morning, which had carried a sharp chill from the east, Jack was on his way out for his walk when he was stopped by a call from down the track. Turning, he saw Vaila in her red raincoat, running with some urgency towards him. She saw him looking and waved one arm in the air. He and Loretta paused by the shed to wait.

'Should you no be at school?' he asked, as she came to a stop in front of them. She reached out towards Loretta, who turned as though offended and slunk into the garden.

'It's only half past seven,' she said.

Jack could have sworn it was later.

'Loretta usually comes for a walk wi me in the mornin,' he told Vaila.

'I know. I want to come with you.'

'How did you ken that?'

'We can see you from our house. We see you all the time.'

This fact struck Jack as peculiar, as though he'd had company without even knowing it.

'Will we be back in time for you to get to school?'

'Mummy said we would if we hurried. She said you're usually gone for forty-five minutes.'

'Huh. Okay, well I guess we should get movin, then.'

Vaila needed some assistance at first. She could not easily cross the fence as Jack did, and nor could she walk between the wires like Loretta. So Jack had to lift her over, and set her down on the other side. She was grinning.

Loretta seemed to recognise that this was an unusual occasion, and she ran ahead of them across the field, then sat waiting like a lookout until they caught up. Once outside the garden, though she liked to be in Jack's company, she always stayed a few metres away, not allowing herself to be touched. Whenever Vaila approached her, she would walk ahead just a little too fast to be caught.

'Dunna mind her,' Jack said. 'She thinks she's a wild animal when she's oot here. Gets all aloof and flighty.'

'What is a loof?' Vaila asked.

Jack laughed. 'It just means she keeps her distance, pretends she doesna ken you. In the hoose she's desperate for cuddles, but oot here she's more of a loner.'

Vaila took this information in. 'Do you think I could train her to like cuddles out here?'

'I dunna think that's the kind of thing you can train a cat to do. Onyway, it's fine for her to be a bit wilder sometimes, don't you think?'

Vaila clearly did not think that, but she gave up trying to convince Loretta to come closer.

When they crossed the second fence at the bottom of the ridge, Jack lifting Vaila to the other side again, the kitten went on ahead. Usually, still, she would turn around at this point, though some days she would sit and wait. Only once in a while did she begin the climb.

Jack and Vaila followed her.

'It's steep, isn't it?' Vaila asked.

'It's no too bad. You've been up here afore, have you no? Wi your mam?'

'No,' she said, shaking her head. This seemed impossible to Jack.

'It's a mountain,' Vaila said, a moment later, as though in explanation. Jack didn't argue.

They took his usual route, the fastest way up, a scant trail made by his own feet in the grass and heather.

When they were halfway, the little girl stopped and took off her raincoat, tucked it under her arm. She wasn't out of breath, but she looked dispirited, as if this were proving to be much more of an effort than she'd imagined. She leaned against a ledge of granite, her face bowed.

'Do you want to go doon again?' Jack asked. He did not want to go back, but the responsibility of Vaila's presence weighed on him.

She shook her head. 'No,' she said. 'But will you hold my hand? You're just going a bit too fast for me.'

Jack considered this: how his long strides had been too much for her, and how he hadn't thought to slow down. 'I'm sorry,' he told her. Then he reached out his hand.

The three of them arrived at the top together, Vaila huffing and puffing extravagantly, as if she had just completed a marathon. The ridge did not have a summit, exactly, it just levelled out into a lumpy plateau of rock and low grass before falling again towards the sea. Jack stopped. Vaila and Loretta stopped, too.

'Wow,' Vaila said, stretching the word out like bubble gum in her mouth. She turned first one way then the other, looking at the shore beyond, then at the fields and buildings behind them. She seemed entirely amazed. 'That's your house,' she said, pointing at Hamar.

'Yes,' Jack said.

'And that's mine.' She pointed at the blue wooden house just beyond.

'Yes,' Jack said again.

'You can see everything from here.'

Jack agreed with her about that. He loved how thrilled she was by this view, this new perspective on her home. He felt the same way. Every morning, he felt the same way.

A raven flew low above them, glancing in their direction, as though surprised to see anyone up here in its territory. It called – a short, guttural bark – and then was gone.

'Why do you come here all the time?' Vaila asked. She was still looking down towards her own house.

Jack shrugged. 'I dunna ken, really,' he said. 'It's just a habit. I like to keep an eye on all this, I guess. Make sure everythin is as it should be. I canna see it all from doon there.'

Vaila seemed satisfied with that answer, even if Jack was not.

'Can we go to the sea?' she asked, turning around to look in the other direction.

'I dunna think we hae time for that. Another mornin we can go, when there's nae school.'

'This weekend maybe?'

'This weekend would be good, yes.' Jack was surprised to find the thought of such an excursion pleasing. 'Maybe your mam would like to come, too.'

Vaila screwed her nose up. 'Mummy doesn't like to walk,' she said.

'Oh. Okay.'

Vaila turned to him, seeming to recognise this as the right moment to pose a question she had been considering for some time. She looked straight at Jack. 'Why are your eyebrows so big?' she asked, a tone of genuine concern in her voice.

Jack raised two fingers to his face, touched the hassock of stiff hair above his right eye. He was amused by the question, but he didn't want Vaila to think he was laughing at her. 'They just keep growin,' he said. 'They used to be like yours: neat and tidy. But as I got aulder, they got bigger.'

'Will mine look like that when I get old?'

169

'No, I dunna think so. And you can cut them if you want, like the hair on your head. I dunna mind them, though. They've never caused me ony bother.'

This time Vaila did not seem quite satisfied, and her face moved as if in search of another question. Jack took his watch out from the inside pocket of his jacket, where it always lived. It was twelve minutes past eight. He felt a quick, sharp panic. 'Come on,' he said, before she had a chance to speak again. 'We need to get doon, or we'll both be in trouble.'

Loretta, as though she understood perfectly what had been said, set off down the slope at jogging pace, soon scampering among the stones. Jack and Vaila followed, as quickly as they were able, the little girl reaching for his hand at the steepest parts of the path.

The next morning – or perhaps it was the one after that – Jack was heading home from his walk, more ravenous than usual. He would make porridge, he thought, as he stepped back into the garden, with a big dollop of syrup in the middle. It was his favourite breakfast by some margin, but he didn't eat it every day. Favourites could be ruined like that, Jack thought. Most days, he had eggs, which was fine, or else toast, which was fine as well. Porridge was something to look forward to. Something to enjoy. This was a day for enjoyment.

He paused in the garden to admire the fattening pods of broad beans, and to watch a bumblebee humming among the flowers in search of nectar. Loretta was on the window ledge outside the living room when he turned the corner.

She had not followed him up the hill that morning. She had plans of her own, it seemed, and had trotted off down the track as soon as he'd opened the door. Jack liked that she had secrets now, a life in which he played no part. He reached out and she thrust her face into his cupped hand, rubbing one cheek then the other against his rough palm. He let her continue for a minute, until she began to tire of the pleasure, then he put his hands around her, just behind her front legs, and picked her up.

Her thin body swung beneath his grip, her back legs and tail dangling. Loretta accepted this indignity. She allowed Jack to pull her close against his chest and to carry her to the porch. She had ceased purring, and her face was no longer one of delight. But she didn't struggle. She trusted him.

The porch door was closed, and Jack turned the handle with one hand, the other still holding the cat to his shoulder. He set her down, and opened the inside door, letting her slink beyond to find her bowl. Then he picked up the white envelope that was lying on the porch floor.

Jack followed the cat to the kitchen. He dropped the envelope on the table, then went to find his glasses from the living room.

There was no stamp on the envelope, and no address – it was too early in the day for post, anyhow. There was just his name, written in large, careful letters. He sat down, opened it, pulled out the card, a photograph of a blackbird on a fence. The message inside was written twice. Once, on the left, in a child's hand: uneven, hesitant, with several spelling mistakes. On the right, an adult had translated, neat and clear. He read both, then read them again.

*Dear Jack. This is an invitation to your birthday party. It will be at 3 p.m. next Saturday at our house. Please tell us what cake you want. We will make it for you. From Vaila.*

Jack put the card down on the table and took his glasses off. He pulled his shirt sleeve down over his right hand, and used the cuff to wipe his eyes.

# LONELY MOUNTAIN

*verse*
I will climb that lonely mountai —
The one that watches over me
I will stand ~~high~~ upon it's shoulders
Just to see what I can see

I have ~~seen~~ had my share of troubles
~~Even when I've~~ ~~tried to hide~~
~~Troubles break so~~
Troubles follow(ed) me around
Some I've buried deep within me
Some I've buried in ~~the~~ this ground

CHORUS

It seems to me that every new day
~~Is Shorter~~ than the one before
goes faster
So many days lie far behind me
~~Into~~ On some cold and foreign shore

CHORUS

I've known pain and I've known ~~trouble~~ sorrow
But my life it has been blessed
There is light with every shadow
I've known love & tenderness

173

# the arrival

## 1975–1978

Change came in the 1970s. It moved slowly at first then accelerated until it was unstoppable. Whispers became rumours became news became a great upheaval, the likes of which no one in the islands had seen before.

Oil is what brought them: the American voices, the English voices, the big ships and the smell of money. Oil.

It'll come to nothing, folk thought, at first. They'll move on, go somewhere else. Somewhere nearer to where they came from, somewhere easier to reach.

But the voices grew louder, and the smell became a stench. Those with influence, with what counted in Shetland for power, opened their arms and, at once, put out their hands. You can come here, they said, but you'll have to make it worth our while, you'll have to do it on our terms. And who would believe it, the gamble worked. The oil companies looked to the government to end this insolence, and the government shrugged, then enshrined the insolence in law. Oil could come to Shetland, but the companies would have to pay for the privilege. They could build, certainly, but only where they were told.

Afraid that such a deal might be repeated elsewhere, the companies very quietly agreed. Just this once, they said. Just this once.

And so the building began.

No one was ever fully sure why Sonny Paton responded to these developments with such anger, such raucous indignation. Not his wife, not his friends, not his son. He whose way in the world had been greased by whale oil, who had built half his home with the money that stinking gloop had brought him, he could not abide the thought of it. A disgrace, he called it. A contemptible disgrace. He had no time for those who praised the representatives of the islands' council, who saw in their actions a shrewd and a plucky defiance. Whores, the lot of them, Sonny said, to whomever would listen. Selling us out for a trickle of black gold.

He wasn't the only one, of course. There were others who felt the same, who feared what might become of the islands' culture and communities, who resented the impositions of this industry, who wanted no part in the great change that was now upon them. Not many, though, expressed their views as vociferously as Sonny.

He developed, at that time, something of a reputation: cantankerous, obstreperous, ungrateful. Before, he was known as a serious man, a man whose words were few but usually worth hearing. He was sensible. Not wise, exactly, but someone who thought before he spoke. Now you could hardly shut him up. He would harangue visitors. The postman heard it many times, neighbours, friends, strangers:

few who came to Hamar escaped it. In the shop or the post office, in the little pub in Treswick, he would rant, repeating the same old complaints, the same old accusations.

Some found his obsession amusing, and would poke and prod him, like a chained bear, enjoying the spectacle of his fury. For Kathleen, it was exhausting. She herself held no strong opinions about the oil terminal at Sullom Voe, other than her opinion that, whatever happened, people like her and Sonny had no ability to change it. The future would be decided elsewhere. There was nothing to be done but to live with it, to get on with things as they were and as they would be. She wished that he would see things the same way.

And anyway, she thought, when her husband's tirades wore her down, what exactly was he afraid of? Of money? Of jobs? Of any change at all? What exactly did he think would be lost?

Sonny would not have found it easy to answer these questions clearly or calmly had his wife ever asked in those terms. The fear he felt – though he did not call it fear – was vague, despite its intensity. The sense he had that loss was part of this bargain with the oil companies, a loss of something that could not be replaced, was more than just a feeling. It was knowledge, certainty. But he could not put into words quite what that loss would be. It was something he had known all his life, some invisible glue that tied the community together, that held one family to another, that fused one person's fate to that of their neighbours. As so often in Sonny's life, it was a lack of definition, of clarity, that heightened and sharpened his anger.

One Saturday night, after several drinks, when Henry, and Henry's wife Laureen, and their nearest neighbours, Old Andrew and Dorothy, were visiting, Sonny blustered as never before. On and on he went that evening, shouting and swearing about the shameless rogues in the Town Hall, banging the base of his glass on the table as he spoke, flecks of spittle like spindrift leaping from the corners of his mouth. The neighbours, having listened long enough, made their excuses and left, and Kathleen stood to tidy bottles and glasses away. Jack went to his room. Throughout the evening, he had looked mortified by his father, who was like some mad old prophet raging at the disobedient ocean.

Words were said. In the kitchen, Henry and Kathleen spoke to Sonny as neither of them had ever spoken to him before. Laureen, too. They told him it must stop. This incessant fury, this pointless fulmination: it must stop. Now.

And stop it did. After that night, Sonny hardly ever spoke of the terminal again. He acted as though he had never even heard of it, as though it were no concern whatsoever of his. It was the strangest kind of relief, Kathleen thought. Like a storm that dies at its most ferocious moment: you could never quite trust that it wasn't coming back.

# 9

Jack found Sarah's landline number in the local phone directory, which was years old now but which he kept, still, on a shelf in the hallway. He disliked speaking on the phone, but as he felt too embarrassed to go and knock on the door – and he didn't want Vaila to overhear him – he would make an exception in this case.

Sarah answered quickly.

'Jack,' she said, when she heard his voice. 'To what do I owe this pleasure?'

'Um,' he said, already a little derailed, 'I wanted to speak aboot the card you sent. Aboot the party.'

'Well, sure, except it wasn't me who sent it. It was Vaila's idea. Both card and party.'

'Yeah, I figured that, which is why I wanted to speak to you.'

'Are you going to tell me you don't want to come to a birthday party planned by a little girl, Jack?' She laughed, as if this were exactly what she was expecting.

'No quite that,' he said, then clarified. 'I mean, no, that wasna what I was going to say.'

'Okay, well, that's good. Vaila will be pleased.'

'Are you sure it's okay, though? That she invited me?'

'Well, I wouldn't have helped her write the card if it wasn't, would I?'

Jack conceded that this was true, and he felt silly for asking. Sarah could do that to him, somehow. She could turn his uncertainties around and make them seem absurd. He liked her for that. There was an odd sort of generosity to it, he thought.

He looked down at his feet, where Loretta was winding herself in a figure of eight between his legs. She wanted something: food, attention. She'd appeared in the hallway as soon as he'd picked up the phone.

'And will it just be us?' Jack asked, then. 'The three of us?'

'Yup. Unless you want to invite anyone else along, which you're welcome to do. Or unless you want Vaila to invite some of her friends, which I would seriously advise against.'

'No, just us is fine.' Jack imagined, with some horror, a room full of small children.

'Good,' she said. 'Great. And about the cake. Do you have a particular preference? Vaila wanted to make a chocolate cake, but that only reflects her own tastes. I told her it should be your favourite, not hers.'

'Well, I dunna really ken,' he said. 'I mean, I dunna want you to go to ony trouble. I'm no needin a cake.'

'It's no trouble. Vaila likes baking, or at least she likes helping me to bake. And so long as it's nothing too fancy we're both perfectly capable. Plus, if it all goes wrong we can just buy something in the shop. No problem.' She let a small sigh slip. 'Look, stop worrying about this, Jack. Vaila is eight years old. There is nothing in the world she likes more than a birthday party. And if it's not her own birthday, then someone else's will do. This will make her very happy, and that makes me happy, and hopefully it'll make you happy, too. It'll be fun. You can come, have a piece of cake, a cup of tea, then head home again. It can be as brief as you like.'

Jack again felt foolish. 'I'm sorry,' he said. 'It was just a bit unexpected. The invitation. The party. I've no paid ony attention to my birthday in aboot forty years, so this was . . . well, I dunna ken, really. I dunna want you to think I'm no grateful. I was pleased to get the card.' He paused to think of a better word. 'I was touched,' he said. 'Very.'

'Good, I'm glad to hear that. Because I don't want it to be a chore for you. You know what I said' – Sarah lowered her voice to a whisper – 'if she gets too much, visits too often, just tell her to ease off, or tell me. It's completely fine. She won't think twice about it. The world is still a mystery to her, so she'll just accept it if I ask her not to bother you for a while. She'll complain for a day or two, then she'll be absolutely fine.'

'The world is still a mystery when you're an auld man,' Jack said.

Sarah laughed. 'Yes, that's true. Not that you're an old man, I mean. But the mystery bit. It doesn't go away, does it?' She laughed again. 'Do you *feel* like an old man?' she asked, after a brief silence. 'Sorry if that's a weird question.

I just think about it sometimes. Some days I look at Vaila and I feel utterly ancient. Other days, I can't believe they allow me to be a mother at all. I feel like a kid behind the wheel of a bulldozer. I'm completely out of my depth.'

Jack made a noise of agreement. 'Yes,' he said. 'I do. I feel like an auld man. But I've felt like that for a long time. Since I was younger as you.' He reached down to pet Loretta, who was lying on her side now in front of him. 'But that's my own fault,' he said.

'Your own fault?' He could hear Sarah smile at this. 'How is getting old your fault?'

'It's not,' he said. 'But *feelin* auld is. That's somethin I let happen. It's like I sat doon and then didna get up again.'

'Hmm,' Sarah replied. 'I think I know what you mean. There's a kind of comfort to it, I imagine.'

'Some days there is,' Jack agreed. He was surprised at the things he would say to Sarah, almost without meaning to.

'Well,' she told him, 'you know what's going to make you feel *really* old? You and me both, in fact. It's a birthday party organised by a little girl.' She cleared her throat and spoke more quietly again. 'Please do not be surprised if this event is not quite to your tastes,' she said. 'But I will do my best to make it fun for everyone, I promise.'

'Thanks,' Jack said. 'I canna wait. And that's the truth.' He tried to think of something else to say. 'Oh, yes,' he remembered. 'Chocolate cake is perfect. It's my favourite, too.'

'Noted,' Sarah said. 'Chocolate cake it is.'

★ ★ ★

Jack had read somewhere that in country songs the past is translated into myth and the present is translated into fiction. Or perhaps he hadn't read that at all. Perhaps it was just something he'd thought, then forgotten, then remembered again, as if it belonged to someone else. He wasn't sure now. And it didn't matter anyway. The fact was that, in songs, there are no true stories. Or all of them are true. The result is just the same. They belong to an alternative world, in which everything and nothing is true at once. To listen to them is to stand before a clear pane, between one world and another, and to gaze through.

The pane plays tricks. In certain lights, it acts like a mirror, reflecting the listener back on themselves. They see their faces, their limbs, their hearts. In other lights, it disappears entirely, and it's possible to imagine that one can reach through – *step* through, even – to that other world. It's possible to imagine that nothing divides one side from the other.

The window, then, is the work of the singer. At least, Jack thinks that must be the case, though he feels something slipping from his grasp as he tries to hold the idea still in his head. The singer's job, their sole purpose, is to keep the pane in place, to hold it up for a few minutes, so the listener can glimpse through, so they can see whatever it is they might want to see.

Singing is a bit like acting, a bit like lying. The task is to convince. It doesn't matter if you've written the words yourself or not, you just have to make them sound like the truth, to create the illusion of honesty.

Jack's metaphor had lost some of its clarity now. It had

become cloudy and warped around the edges. But it still felt near enough coherent.

There were, he thought, two kinds of art in music, two kinds of artifice: writing and performance. A mediocre song could be brought to life by the right singer, and a good song could survive even the most slapdash of performances.

This made it hard to speak of a song as singular. It was not an object, like a book or a shovel. It had a different kind of life. Or lives, really. A song was more like . . . Jack searched for the right analogy but came up only with the wrong one: a hand puppet. That was a weird comparison. Unsatisfying. He tried to step backwards, onto solid ground. A song was more like . . .

There was a chill in the breeze again that afternoon, which Jack had pushed firmly from his thoughts for several minutes, but which now was nudging at him, demanding attention. He looked down at Loretta, who was curled up asleep on the bench beside him. He placed his hand on her belly, and she flinched, then stretched and yawned, without opening her eyes. She recognised the hand.

Jack tried again to resurrect the idea: the two worlds divided by a window, the illusion of honesty, the double life of a song. He tried to hold it all aloft and to push it towards some kind of conclusion, to really make sense of it. But all he could think of now was a puppet, a sad little puppet with a wooden head and a scarlet gown, like the star of a Punch and Judy show. Then he was thinking of one puppet hitting another with a stick. He was thinking of a baby and a crocodile and a string of sausages. It was all over.

Jack was often frustrated by his inability to pull thoughts neatly together. So often, like this, he would follow an idea some distance, only to have it fall apart on him unfinished. His head was a mess.

Earlier, he had been listening to songs about lost love. He'd been chopping and changing, pulling one CD out of the machine and swapping it for another, then another, as if there were something in particular he was looking for. But there wasn't.

He'd been thinking as he listened how different it was to judge a song than to judge a performance, how the quality of one could be *heard* but the other had to be *felt*.

He'd listened to Ernest Tubb: that deep and mellifluous delivery. If he was feeling loss, you couldn't really tell. He'd listened to Jerry Lee Lewis, who sounded like a caged animal, magnificent and dangerous. He'd listened to Kitty Wells, who could be defiant and vulnerable all at once, exuberant and yet on the very edge of tears. He'd listened to Gram Parsons, whose voice seemed to carry pain, no matter what he sang about. He'd listened to Floyd Tillman, who sounded drunk and in denial. Maybe it wasn't like acting at all, then. A singer didn't need to play the character of the song, they didn't need to weep and wail in order to demonstrate hurt. It was something else.

It was possible to sing flippantly about heartbreak, to make light of loss, and yet still convey it. It was possible to infuse every word with torment and longing. It was possible to sound unmoved, and yet still make a listener cry. It was something about tone, Jack thought. Something about enunciation. Something about breath. Something about expression and restraint. It was not acting but *inhabiting*. The good singer lives inside a song. For a few minutes they are nowhere else.

So maybe it *was* like puppetry after all.

Loretta made a noise like a squeak, a reminder to the hand to keep scratching.

Jack had no idea if he was a good singer or not. Someone else would have to tell him, and there was no one who could do that.

It wasn't often that Jack stood like this, in front of the mirror, looking at himself. Most days he wouldn't see his own reflection at all, unless he happened to catch a glimpse in a window, or in the rearview of the car. His appearance always came as something of a surprise to him, his face no longer one with which he was completely familiar. When he really stopped and looked, as he did now, he felt the need to prod at himself, as if to check that everything he saw was really him.

He turned one way then the other, patted the shirt down on his belly. When he stood side-on, the belly protruded. There was no getting around that. With the shirt untucked, it was better, less obvious, but it couldn't be hidden. The shirt had been bought when the belly was smaller, and if he were buying it now he'd go a size up – for comfort, and to conceal himself better. But it did still fit, just about.

It was his best shirt: midnight blue, Western-style, with white stitching on the shoulders, chest pockets and collar. Other than a small embroidered pattern – vaguely botanical – on the cuffs and collar, and the pearl popper buttons,

185

there was nothing especially fancy about it. But you could tell the quality was good. You could tell it wasn't cheap.

Jack had bought it on a whim about ten years ago – together with the hat that hung behind his bedroom door – from an online company that specialised in Western clothing. It was the first time he'd purchased something from the internet, and it felt, in every way, extravagant. The shop had everything: cowboy boots, check shirts, fringed trousers, even suits encrusted with rhinestones. Jack's choice had been on the conservative side, as far as the range of possible options went. But the inexplicable impulse on which he had acted in buying it had been entirely out of character. He had nowhere to wear it, after all. Other than one time, shortly after it arrived, when he put overalls and a thick coat on top of it and went to the shop, this would be the first time the shirt had left the house.

The birthday party was not an occasion for dressing up. Sarah had made that clear. He was to take nothing with him and to make no effort, she said. She and Vaila had everything under control. But he wanted to show them that the invitation mattered, that he appreciated it and took it seriously, in the best of ways. He wanted to make just this one small bit of effort.

And so here he was, in his spare bedroom, in front of the mirror on his mother's old dressing table. He had trimmed his beard, washed his hair, even *combed* his hair. And though he felt somewhat foolish for doing so, he also felt pleased. Vaila and Sarah would not laugh at his shirt, and they would probably not even notice his belly. They wouldn't judge him for it, anyway. They wouldn't care.

Jack tried to remember the last time he'd attended a birthday party. It might have been his cousin's fiftieth, in Lerwick, almost a decade ago. He'd gone, then, out of a sense of familial obligation. He and his cousin were a few years apart in age, and unalike in temperament. They had never been close. Jack had stood in the corner of the living room with a bottle of beer warming in his hands for the best part of two hours. People nodded hello to him, and a few – those he knew by name – asked how he was doing. His cousin's wife had stopped to chat for a few minutes, then had patted his shoulder and moved on. Jack had felt very alone that day. He had left while most of the guests were still sober.

It wasn't that he disliked people. He was unsociable, not misanthropic. He chose to avoid situations in which he was likely to feel stranded, isolated. Which meant, very often, that he avoided the company of others. Some might think that ironic, but for Jack, well, it was what it was and that was that.

He loosened his belt – no point being uncomfortable – then turned away from the mirror and into the living room. It was still too early to leave, even if he strolled at a snail's pace down the track, so he sat in his armchair, then stood, went to the kitchen, poured himself a glass of water, then sat again. Loretta was eyeing him from the sofa. She could tell something was up, he thought; she could sense his anticipation. He wondered if he ought to bring her with him. Vaila would like that. But Sarah might not approve. And the cat herself would likely object to being dragged into someone else's house. It was a bad idea.

He leaned back, looked up at the ceiling. There was a cluster of cobwebs in the far corner of the room, and a string of spider silk dangled beneath it like the tail of a kite, moved by a breath of air too subtle for Jack to feel. How long had that been there, he wondered. He had plenty of time to get rid of it now, to pull the vacuum cleaner out of the cupboard and hold the nozzle in the air. But Loretta hated the hoover. She would run, terrified, for the door, and he didn't want to disturb her. He used it less often now that she was here, and the house was not as clean as he liked it to be. There were fine black hairs on the furniture and the carpet. Tomorrow he would deal with it.

He stood again, swigged back the rest of the water and checked the clock on the kitchen wall. Twenty-five to three. He could make a cup of tea, but his bladder already felt full.

He went to the toilet.

Twenty-two minutes to three.

He could listen to a couple of songs, perhaps, but there was nothing he wanted to hear. He glanced at the wall of music, but no. He was too distracted.

'Right, then,' he said, and the cat looked up. 'Just aboot time to make a move.' He brushed his hands down his shirt again, smoothing away invisible wrinkles.

Loretta yawned, stretched her front paws out, then hopped – almost fell, really – from the sofa to the floor. She ambled to the kitchen, leaned into her bowl and took a biscuit in her mouth. Jack heard it shatter between her teeth, then heard several more go the same way. She lapped at the water in the other bowl, then wandered past him towards the door.

'Oh, you're comin too, then, are you?' Jack said. He didn't usually speak to the cat quite this much. 'Let's be off, then.' He looked at the clock for a third time. Seventeen minutes to three.

Jack and Loretta walked together down the track. The afternoon was mild. For several days prior, it had rained almost without pause. Easterly gusts had spattered the windows for hour after hour. But today it was dry, and Jack didn't wear a coat.

The cat was easily distracted. She followed the edge of the grass verge, sometimes jumping up to higher ground near the fence, then down again, into the dry ditch that ran between.

'I did a fine job of this,' Jack said, kicking at the loose stones on the track's flat surface. 'Looks good. Maybe I should do it for a livin,' he laughed. 'Plenty of potholes to fill aroond here.'

Loretta did not reply, but she did glance up at him every once in a while.

'They'll no mind me bein early,' Jack said.

Loretta then did something he had not seen her do before. She leapt out of the ditch, up to the high point of the verge, then up again, to the top of a fencepost, where she stood, as though it were the most natural place in the world for her to be.

Jack turned to look at her. He wondered if she'd done this before, or if she were trying it out for the first time. And he thought to himself, then, what an extraordinary

thing a cat was. What a marvellous thing this particular cat
– *his* cat – was.

Loretta stood, seeming to accept his admiration for a
moment, then hopped off the fence post again and trotted
onward down the track. She had a purpose now, and Jack
followed close behind her until he reached Sarah and Vaila's
house. From there, Loretta continued towards the road,
paying him no more attention.

Jack climbed the steps towards the front door, taking them
slowly, his hand on the wooden rail, painted the same rich
blue as the house. He reached the top, still holding the rail,
and he moved towards the front door. And then he stopped.

When he thought back to that moment, as he did many
times in the days and nights that followed, over and over
and over, he could not be certain what it was exactly that
he heard, what it was that alerted him. Did he hear the
car approach on the main road, unseen behind the house?
Did he hear the driver press the brakes, too late, the tight
shriek of tyres? What was it? He couldn't say. In his mind,
it was not a sound that made him turn his head, it was
just a word. *Loretta.*

Jack ran. He jumped the bottom three steps, then hauled
the gate wide open. He ran, certain already of what he was
running towards, knowing already what he would find
when he got there. He ran, and felt a sharpness rise in his
lungs, and then a sickening calm. And in that instant of
calm he saw the kitten, perched atop another fence post,
cleaning herself, her one white paw held up as though to
keep it safe and dry, and he saw beyond her, flat on the
tarmac of the road, a bright red raincoat.

The driver was still inside the car when Jack reached the girl. He felt the heat of the engine on his cheek as he leaned towards her. He touched his hand to Vaila's face. Her eyes were closed, her mouth open. Tiny splinters of gravel were stuck to her lower lip. He leaned in closer, but he was shaking too much to see if she was breathing. He put two fingers to her neck, tried to concentrate, to close out all other senses, but he couldn't find a pulse. He couldn't be certain. His body screamed. His ears felt full, like he was under water. His heart clattered against his ribs, as though trying to escape.

'Ambulance!' he called out, in a voice that didn't sound like his own. High-pitched. Half-strangled. As he looked up he saw the driver just behind him now, with a phone already to his ear. The man was familiar, Jack thought. He knew his face, and found himself hunting through his memory for a name. Nothing came to him.

He turned back.

Vaila was curled on her right side, just in front of the car's bumper. Around her, stalks of angelica were scattered on the road, but Jack didn't stop, then, to consider why. He could see no blood. Not on her face or her hands. Aside from the position of her legs, which were twisted one over the other, she looked almost comfortable, as if she might be sleeping. Jack knew not to move her, though. He knew to keep her still.

He tried to focus, and watched her chest, lifting the raincoat away so he could see better.

A breath.

Another breath.

He moved his head close, felt the bottom button of his shirt pop open against the strain of his stomach. He whispered to her: 'Vaila, Vaila, can you hear me?' He pulled her hair back from her face, and saw a little white piece of plastic, a wireless earphone, nestled inside her ear. He plucked it out and spoke again.

She made no sound.

The driver was at his shoulder now, leaning in. 'She jumped oot from the verge,' the man said, his voice quaking. 'She wasna lookin.' Jack waved him away with one arm. He moved his body forward as if to shelter her, as if he could protect her now from what had already happened, from the damage she had already sustained.

He bowed his head and saw another breath, the faintest movement of her lips.

And as he leaned over her like that, watching, listening, Jack heard a sound from behind him that made his own lungs tighten, his limbs near enough give way. It was a noise like torn metal, like glass stretched and severed; it was a wail that cleaved through the August air. He turned towards Sarah, who was running, and put his hand out to slow her, to stop her from grabbing the girl, to stop her from lifting the girl from the road. He pressed hard against her, absorbed the force of her motion, and for a few seconds, until she knelt down beside him, the weight of her body against his arm, he held Sarah and Vaila apart.

# I miss you today

I miss.
I've ~~been missing~~ you today
I've been lost and on my own / all alone?
I've been talking to myself
About the love that I have known

It's a bargain ~~that~~ we (both) made
wouldn't have it any other way
we met, we loved, and ~~then~~ we parted
And I miss you today

hurt
There's a pain that never leaves me
~~It lingers~~ There's a hunger in my blood
There's a thirsting in my heart
Ever/since (the day) ~~so~~ we've been apart

I can't tell you how it feels / I feel
It's impossible to say
But I just wanted you to know
That I miss you today

                    Rpt after break!

193

# the dissuasion

## 1979–1981

It had been obvious for some time, years really, that Jack
was not inclined to work the croft with his father. As
a teenager, he would help out when asked, and he would
do so without too much grumbling. He didn't seem to
mind the work. But nor did he have any real enthusiasm
or aptitude for it. He had not inherited Sonny's sense of
determination or of duty towards the place. He did what
he was told and no more, and Sonny would often have
to watch over his shoulder to make sure Jack was doing
it right.

This was a source of only minor disappointment, and
even then only to his father. Life was different now. There
was no ignoring that. Shetland was full to bursting with
work. There were jobs for anyone who wanted them. Sonny
himself was only a weekend crofter by then. He worked
for the county during the week, as part of a road crew,
widening and resurfacing the byways of the islands. Most
people drove by then, so the road work never ended.

And anyway, Sonny was only just past forty, that was all. He was a young man, strong, healthy. He had no need to think about passing the place on. Not for a long time. Jack had years, decades, to change his mind.

The bigger problem, as far as his parents were concerned, was that Jack's mind was never really fixed on anything in particular. Not in terms of work, anyway. He was bright, that was clear, but he hadn't applied himself in school, and so when it came time to leave he could not have gone to college or university, as some of his peers had done, even if he'd wanted to. He didn't have the grades. Jack read books, he listened to music, he played the guitar, he helped out when he was needed. Kathleen didn't doubt he would have gone on like that if they'd let him. He was a drifter by inclination, not a swimmer.

Sonny had never been as stern or severe a parent as some might have expected him to be − and he was less harsh by far than his own father had been − but here he drew a line. Drifting wasn't good enough. Not at Jack's age. 'He's eighteen, for goodness' sake!' (Kathleen knew exactly what was coming next when Sonny spoke those particular words.) He, Sonny, had been in the Antarctic when he was that age, working till his hands were raw, knee-deep in blubber and blood, and all for a pocketful of change. Kathleen was well aware that, for most of his time as a whaler, her husband had worked in the ship's mess, and that, while he'd surely helped to cut and cook the meat often enough, he'd rarely been knee-deep in blubber. She knew, too − because he once had told her this − that in some indeterminable way, Sonny felt scarred by his time at the whaling, that he felt none of the wistfulness for that time with which some of his former colleagues still spoke. But she knew, most of all, not to contradict him.

'If he'll no swim of his own accord,' said Sonny, 'then what he needs is a push. He can stay in the hoose if he wants, but from now on he'll pay for his food and his share of the bills. And for that, he'll need a job.'

Kathleen was torn. She didn't disagree with her husband. Jack could not continue to hang around the house like this. He needed to do something. But she favoured a nudge over a push. She worried that, without help, he would make the wrong decision, go in the wrong direction. 'Can you no put in a word for him?' she asked. 'Find him a job wi the coonty?' Sonny agreed that he could.

Jack, predictably, did not want a job fixing roads or building council houses. He wasn't cut out for either. He considered going to Sullom Voe, to the oil terminal; there was plenty of work there. But the principal appeal of that was only to annoy his father, which wasn't a good enough reason in the end. And so, after as much dithering as he could get away with, Jack went to work in the storeroom of a company that supplied fresh food to some of the smaller shops around the islands. It was menial work. He checked the deliveries that came off the ferry in the morning. He checked the orders from the shops, and made sure they got what they needed. He was good at it, without ever being too good. When the job of storeroom manager came up a year after he started, nobody even thought to ask Jack if he wanted it.

If anything, Kathleen worried more once Jack was working than she had before he started. It was a gnawing, niggling worry that grew as the months went on. There was a freedom then in the islands that had not existed when she and Sonny were young. It was a freedom to choose, to some extent, the kind of future, the kind of life, that you wanted. There were jobs that had never existed before. There were opportunities to make money. There was a sense of growth and expansion. Her son was clever – more clever than either of his parents, she thought – and yet he showed no interest in using his mind, in making the most of the opportunities around him. He seemed more or less content with his storeroom job, earning little, going nowhere.

But it was more than that. It was never just the job. Jack's world seemed too small to Kathleen. He was twenty now, and he still spent almost every evening at home with his parents. He had few friends – that much had never changed – and the only socialising he did, at least that she knew of, was to drink an occasional pint with his colleagues on a Saturday afternoon before he caught the bus back home. She saw a lack in him, in the way he lived, and his failure to push against that lack concerned her. The only direction in which his effort, his energy, ever really went was towards his guitar.

This was not a worry that Sonny shared, though he did not deny his wife's observations. The boy was working now – that was good – and he wasn't miserable, so far as they could tell. They should be glad of that. Life has a way of throwing things at you, Sonny believed, and if you don't make choices of your own, sooner or later they'll be made regardless. 'Somethin'll happen,' he said. 'Jack'll get bored and find another job. He'll fall in wi some new friends. Maybe even fall in love.' Kathleen raised her eyebrows at that, almost laughed, and then was struck silent. The thought of Jack in love seemed so unlikely to her, so distant, that it brought a sadness to her heart that she could hardly contain.

Oh, Jack!

But what was also true, despite these worries, was that, in other ways, Kathleen was happier then than she had been in years. Happier than she had been since Tom died, more than a decade before. The striving that once had driven her, that once had forced almost every decision that she and her husband made, was all but gone. They weren't getting rich, not like some, but they didn't need to struggle so much any more. They were getting comfortable. And with Jack bringing in wages of his own now, they were better off than they could ever have imagined being. Kathleen felt a lessening of pressure inside her, as if she had sprung some kind of leak. She could breathe more easily, she could let herself relax, and she saw the same slow change in her husband. The times were good for Sonny, much as he had railed against their coming. He didn't love his job, but he liked the men he worked with, and he seemed to find more pleasure in the croft these days as well. It was as if he'd just realised that he enjoyed it: working with the sheep, maintaining the walls and fences, planting and harvesting. He would come in some evenings, filthy and exhausted from work, and he would tuck the hair behind Kathleen's ear and kiss her on the cheek. There was a gentleness in Sonny, then, that she had never quite known before.

Ah, but Jack!

What happened next was that Henry – still Sonny's closest friend – broke his ankle. It was a stupid accident. 'Typical Henry,' Kathleen said, which was somewhat unfair. He was getting out of his tractor – a new one, to him – and he wasn't paying enough attention. His foot slipped on the top step, just as he was launching himself towards the ground, and it caught firmly behind the rung. His forward momentum continued, and he heard the bone snap in the same instant that the pain struck him. He dangled, briefly, head to the ground, until, with an agonising twist, the step let him go. Henry's screams reached halfway to Treswick.

For many weeks afterwards, help was needed. Henry's wife Laureen and his girls, Vina and Ann, would all lend a hand with the feeding, while he hobbled behind them on his cast, shouting instructions, sometimes waving a walking stick in the air. But there was other work to be done, maintenance and repairs, preparation for lambing. And there was Henry's old ram, which neither the girls nor Laureen would go near – and with good reason. A more cantankerous and demanding creature would be hard to imagine.

It was Sonny who volunteered Jack to help out – an odd choice, in some ways, since the boy was far from the most practical person around. But Sonny himself was too busy to offer more than an hour here or there to his friend, and so he offered the only other thing he could think of: his son. Jack did not seem enthusiastic about this arrangement, but nor did he refuse. Doing so, anyway, would have been futile. The decision had been made.

And so, every Sunday after that, Jack became Henry's assistant, his surrogate, working as many hours as he was required. Henry was well aware that Jack was not like his father when it came to hard work, but he also knew a good deal when he saw one, and free labour once a week was a good deal. The only payment Jack received for his labour was lunch, which he ate with the family. Work stopped at a quarter to one, and by the time the men had taken off their jackets in the porch and washed their hands in the bathroom sink, food would be on the table.

They could be noisy, these meals. Henry was a talkative man, and his wife and daughters were no different. They were bright and chatty, all of them, and they never missed an opportunity to contribute. For the most part, they enjoyed each other's company. Disagreements could erupt, but they were generally good-natured, and a laugh from one or other of the girls would quell any dispute. Between one mouthful and the next, tension could rise, peak, and be defused.

These Sunday meals meant a lot to Henry. He felt, always, a pride at mealtimes. He felt pride in his two daughters and his wife; pride in his house, which was cluttered and busy with belongings; and pride in the meal itself, cooked by Laureen and, often as not, the product of their own croft. Henry was a man as near to happy as anyone ever had been. He liked to have guests there to observe the goodness of his life. Even a guest as awkward and as quiet as Jack.

He was a good lad, the Paton boy, nobody would deny that, and Henry thought of him as something like a nephew.

He'd known him since he was a baby, after all. But Lord, it wasn't easy to get a conversation out of him. Outside, Jack would speak comfortably enough about what needed doing – and then would slip into humming as he worked – but at the table, well, that was a different matter. Always, he said thank you for his food, told Laureen how much he enjoyed it. But every word beyond that was a struggle. Ask him a question directly and he would look at his plate, mumble his response as briefly and quietly as he was able. Mostly, he just listened, and seemed happy enough to do so, to be among the family.

It was after six weeks or so, eight maybe, that Henry noticed a change in the boy, in the way he acted at the table, and with Vina in particular. Small things: the way he would turn his head to look and listen when she spoke, the way he nodded at whatever opinion she expressed (and Vina had plenty of those). It was a certain kind of attention he paid her. Subtle, sure. But Henry, who considered himself an observant man, had noticed.

He shared his suspicions with Laureen, and she was sceptical. Jack and Vina had known each other since they were very small. They had played together sometimes when they were young, then lost interest as they got older. They'd been friendly enough over the years, but no more than that. Nothing had suggested to Laureen that things were different now.

And besides, this was Jack they were speaking about. *Jack*, for goodness' sake. The only thing he ever showed enthusiasm for was his guitar – Henry's old one, that was. And even then he would only play it behind his bedroom door.

No amount of cajoling could convince him to bring it out when guests were at Hamar. Laureen shook her head. Her husband was mistaken.

The next weekend, though, she changed her mind. It annoyed her that Henry had seen it first, but he wasn't wrong. There was definitely something, some hint of heedfulness towards the girl. There were glances across the table. And the funny thing: it wasn't just him. Laureen twice caught Vina looking at Jack, and both times the girl turned her head as soon as she was noticed. That wasn't like her at all. Vina was Jack's opposite. She was self-assured – gregarious, even. She wasn't exactly rebellious, other than staying out with friends later than she'd agreed, but she had an independence of spirit that pleased Laureen. She could think for herself. She was the kind of child – and she wasn't a child any more, of course, she was nineteen – that a parent could have confidence in. Confidence that she would find her way in the world, that she would make good decisions for herself.

But was Jack a good decision?

They spoke about it, Laureen and Henry, lying next to each other in the dark. They considered the possibility. She could do worse, they both agreed. He was a fine enough lad. Bright too, not that it was easy to tell. But there was something not quite all there about Jack. That's how Henry put it, whispering his concerns from his side of the bed to hers. The boy's unreachable, he said. It's like he's hiding from the world.

Laureen did not disagree. She was as fond of Jack as her husband was, but the thought of him and her daughter together just didn't sit right with her. He was so unambitious, she thought, so half-hearted in everything he did – except his music, and what good was that? Laureen could not imagine him making something of himself. She could see him doing the same untaxing job until it came time to retire. She could see him sleeping in his childhood bedroom for the rest of his life.

Their daughter could do worse, yes, but she could do better too.

Of course, they were getting ahead of themselves. All they'd seen so far were glances, and knowing Jack it would never get beyond that. He wouldn't pluck up the courage even to speak to Vina away from the kitchen table. And if she spoke to him first he'd probably run a mile.

Henry thought a lot about this as the days went on. More than he needed to. He turned it over in his mind, worrying at it like a pebble in his pocket. He felt a sense of disloyalty over what he'd said and thought – disloyalty to Jack, and to Sonny, his friend. He wondered what Sonny and Kathleen would think if they knew. Likely, they'd be pleased. Vina could bring Jack out of his shell, they might think, show him there's more to life than music. And Henry had considered that, too. The pair of them could be good for each other. Opposites, and all that. And wouldn't it be fine if . . . Ah, but then – he jumped ahead further – what if it all fell apart? What a mess that would be for everyone. What an ugly, awkward mess. Once again, Henry was certain. The potential for disaster was too great. Better for it not to begin at all. At least then he could stop fretting about it.

It was 1981. Parents did not get to choose who their children took a fancy to. Especially not a child like Vina. If that girl got something in her head, in her heart, well, thought Henry, there'd be no dissuading her. He felt an urgency then. If there was dissuasion to be done, he realised, it would have to be aimed at Jack.

The following Sunday, any lingering doubt was gone. The glances, though still furtive, were regular now. They were catching each other's eyes, and smiling between mouthfuls. Smiling! Jack looked positively puppy-eyed.

Henry knew he would need to act.

They were in the big shed that afternoon, he and Jack, just tidying up before the spring really got going. It was late March, then, and you could feel it, the change. Though it was still cold, still wet, still dark, you could feel it coming. Henry was sat on a low, three-legged stool, with his foot on an upturned bucket, watching as Jack gathered tools from wherever they'd been abandoned, putting them back into some kind of order. Over there, Henry would say, pointing. Hang it by the door! Stick that one on the bench. There should be another one in here somewhere.

He was putting the conversation off, naturally, but he couldn't do so for long. He would just have to start talking, he realised, or else it would never happen.

'Jackie!' he said, without any response from the boy. Then again, louder: 'Jackie!'

Jack was half a dozen metres away, in the middle of the shed, with a lump hammer in his hand. 'Where do you want this?' he asked.

'Nowhere for the moment,' Henry replied. 'Just hold on

to it while I say somethin. Or put it doon, it doesna matter.'
He cleared his throat.

Jack held on to the hammer.

'So,' Henry said, 'I couldna help but notice . . . I mean,
Laureen and me, we both noticed that you've been enjoyin
your meals here at the hoose, and I'm pleased aboot that.'

Jack nodded, and Henry cleared his throat again.

'You ken, we both think of you like family. Laureen and
me . . .' Henry's voice trailed off. 'We think of you and
Vina as somethin like cousins. Does that make sense?'

Jack made a face to show that, while it didn't yet make
sense, he was nervous about what might be coming next.

Henry sighed. 'What I mean to say is that we noticed,
both of us, that you and Vina seem to be gettin on well
together. You seem to like each other.'

Now Jack blushed. He turned his head, but there was
no way to hide the scarlet in his cheeks. He looked down
at the hammer in his hand, and kept his eyes focused there,
his shoulders slumped forward.

'Obviously,' said Henry, 'I'm glad you twa get on. That's
a fine thing. But I just think, *we* think, that you shouldna
try to make it ony more as that. Friends is fine, but more
as friends' – he looked up – 'well, it's just no a good idea.
No a good idea at all. It wouldna be right. For you. For
Vina. For onybody.'

For the rest of his life, Henry would remember the way
Jack looked at him then. It was a look of embarrassment,
certainly, of humiliation. But it was more than that. The
boy stood there as though the hammer in his hands weighed
more than he could possibly carry, as though his legs might

be about to buckle, as though some tiny glimmer of hope he had been following had just guttered out.

Henry forced a breath from between his closed lips. He wished already that he hadn't said a word.

Jack did not return the next Sunday, or the Sunday after that. He didn't come back to the house at all. Henry's ankle was much improved by then, and so he managed well enough. He said nothing to Sonny about what had happened, and he hoped — assumed — that Jack would say nothing either. Vina asked where Jack had got to, and Henry could see, could hear in her voice, that the disappointment was mutual. His words had hurt everyone. He would hold that guilt for ever.

It was Sonny, soon after, who told him that Jack was moving to Glasgow.

# 10

It was amazing, Jack thought, just how quiet it could be sometimes. There was nearly always something making noise. He would wake to the grumbling of sheep, or the calls of crows and gulls. He would hear dogs barking, or a vehicle in motion. He would hear the wind. So often just the wind. But this morning there was nothing. No sound. Even Loretta had not yet nosed her way into his room. Jack could hear nothing. It was as though every living thing on this island was keeping still, as he was, just listening, listening, listening. There was nothing to hear.

Jack sometimes had nightmares about going deaf, about the world growing silent. Since most of the pleasure in his life arrived through his ears, it seemed about the worst fate he could think of.

But silence is like a vacuum. It draws in sound. Imagined sound. Remembered sound. Lying there in his bed, looking at a square of white sky through the window, Jack recalled the awful noises of two days before. The sound of the car coming to a stop. The sound of Sarah wailing. The sound of the ambulance hurtling up the narrow road. The sound of a police car and of people asking questions. The sound of the ambulance leaving again, with Sarah and Vaila inside. When he tried to picture it, everything was indistinct. He could hardly conjure a single moment. But he could hear it. He could hear all of it again. Even the sound of his own footsteps as he'd walked home, back up the gravel track, with Loretta following, was clear to him still.

Jack hadn't slept since that evening. Or if he had then he hadn't noticed himself waking again. He just felt dazed, permanently. He lay down and got up again. He walked around the house. He had eaten, but not much.

And there was Loretta now, at the door. She pushed her way through then stood at the foot at the bed, looking up at him. Jack wondered if she could tell that something was wrong, or if she was just being quiet because he was quiet. She kept looking, waiting. He sighed, swung his legs out over the edge of the bed and stood up. He was in an old white T-shirt and red checked pyjama bottoms. He followed the cat to the kitchen.

Vaila was in Aberdeen. She'd not been taken to the hospital in Lerwick, but had instead been driven to an ambulance plane at the airport, and flown away from Shetland. They couldn't tell what internal injuries she might have, so they assumed the worst. Jack knew nothing more. He had heard that much from Vina on the evening of the accident. She'd called him late on to ask how he was, had offered to bring food round for him, to cook something if he needed. He turned her down. He couldn't face seeing anyone that day, or the next. What Vina knew she had heard from a friend of Sarah's, and she wanted to fill in the blanks in her own knowledge. She wanted a first-hand account. Jack had not been able to tell her much.

He was waiting now to hear more, but he didn't know who from. He had tried to call the hospital on the morning after the crash, but when they asked if he was a relative he'd had to say no. And that was the end of that. He didn't have Sarah's mobile number, and he wouldn't have dared to bother her even if he had.

So he was waiting.

Waiting.

Loretta looked up at him again, this time from her food bowl. He was pacing the kitchen, and his anxious movements were disturbing her meal. Her tail swept sideways across the lino, expressing her displeasure.

Jack turned for the door. He would go to the shop. Vina would surely have heard something more by now; she was his best hope for news. He strode out to the porch, and to the front step, then stopped. He was still in his pyjamas, and he had no idea what time it was. He went back inside, and was surprised to see it was already 11 a.m. Perhaps he had slept after all, having lain awake until the early hours. He pulled on a pair of jeans, put a jumper over the T-shirt, found his car keys, and set off again.

The shop was busy when he got there. Two cars outside. He could see people milling through the window. He stayed where he was. He couldn't face strangers now. Vina he could manage.

It was several minutes before the first person came out of the shop and into their car. Jack didn't recognise them, but he put his head down anyway, and pretended to be looking at his phone. Another five minutes and the door opened again. This time it was a couple, Annie and Graham, who lived a mile or two further down the road. He pulled the phone to his ear, and pretended to talk. He waved when they looked his way, and he waited for them to go.

Vina must have seen him coming. Perhaps she'd seen his car arrive and knew that he was waiting. She was at the door when he went in, and she put her arms around him. He had not expected that, and he had not expected the choke of grief in his throat as he felt her hands on his back.

'Ach, Jackie,' she said, as she pulled away. 'How're you keepin?'

He shook his head. 'Ony news?'

'No much,' she told him. 'Nothin, really. Just that she's still there. She had some kind of operation yesterday. That's what Linda thought, but she wasna sure. Naebody seems to ken a thing.' She stepped back just a little. 'I thought Sarah woulda called you by now.'

He shook his again. 'Why would she?' he said. 'It's my fault it happened.'

'Your fault? What are you talkin aboot? It wasna you that was drivin.'

'No,' Jack said, 'but Vaila' – he caught his breath – 'she was collectin flowers for me. For my birthday.' He had realised this only in retrospect. Those angelica stems, scattered.

Vina paused to take this in. 'Jesus, Jackie.' She puffed her cheeks and blew the air out. 'That's terrible. Bloody terrible.

But it's still no your fault.' She put one hand up to his shoulder. 'The only man that's at fault was him behind the wheel. That idiot, Frankie, used to live up the road here' – she pointed with her thumb. 'What in the hell was he doin, speedin along there like that?'

Jack's stomach felt as though it had been wrung out.

'Do you need to sit?' Vina asked, seeing him wobble on his feet.

'No,' Jack said. 'I'll get home. I just need to get home. Call me if there's news, though. Onything at all.' He turned to the door, and heard the bell ring above his head.

They returned two days later. Vaila and Sarah, with Vaila's father, Gary, too. Jack saw them from the window that morning. They must have come back on the first flight. He saw a car arrive, saw two adults get out of the front. Then, a moment later, a little bundle emerged from the back seat, not carried, but shepherded towards the house, her father's arm around her. She was wrapped in some kind of blanket. Swaddled. And still she looked so small. Jack wondered if they'd had to cut the raincoat off her.

From that distance, he couldn't see the cast that he knew was there. A broken arm, plus three fractured ribs, some cuts and bruises. There had been no operation, after all. The doctors had worried about concussion, about internal injuries. But she was okay. She was frail and hurting, but okay.

It was Vina, again, who had told him this. She'd called the day before, had scolded him for not phoning Sarah – Vina had written the number down for him on the back of a receipt – and recounted the extent of what she knew. 'They'll be back tomorrow or the day after,' she said. 'You should visit, they'll want to see you.'

Jack did not believe that. They would not want to see him. Even if Sarah had not blamed him for the accident, she would be angry at him now for his silence, his absence. He had cowered in a corner for too long, and he could see no escape. It was the way things always were.

He turned back to the living room, nauseated, muddled, everything unstraight. He sat beside Loretta on the sofa – she was cleaning herself, taking time over the act – and he felt a geyser of self-disgust rising inside. Jack was a sorry excuse for a man. A waste of space. A waste of everything, really. Decade after decade, he had allowed himself to shrivel, had let his days spill like seeds onto concrete, a hopeless squandering of a life. He was hardly a man at all.

He wanted to throw something, to shout or scream, to thump his fist into the furniture. But he didn't want to scare the kitten. He stood up and went to the spare room, took a pillow from the single bed and grasped his fists around it as tightly as he was able, until his knuckles were bone white and his fingers ached to be released.

He set the pillow back, and straightened the cover on the duvet. On the sofa, the kitten was readying herself to sleep.

In the days that followed, Jack mostly hid at home. He took his walks early in the morning and went to work late in the evening. Other than that he barely left the house at all. He sat around doing next to nothing. The garden went unattended. Even music couldn't reach him. Jack was sick of himself, that was the truth. He was sick of who he had become – of who, perhaps, he had always been.

A week passed. Vaila's father had gone again. Jack saw him leave one morning in a taxi and not return, but he saw no more sign of Sarah or of Vaila. Finally, unable to stomach his own inaction any longer, he resolved to do something worthwhile, something good. That afternoon, in the wake of a heavy rain shower, he stopped his car in front of Sarah's house. He pulled the handbrake and set the gearstick in neutral. But he kept the engine running. He needed to get away quickly once this was done. He couldn't pause.

He looked over at the passenger seat, at the square cardboard box beside him. The box that held Loretta. He put one hand on top of it, as if to brush dust away, then opened his door and reached back towards it.

She had been remarkably quiet so far, trusting him not to harm her. When he first placed her inside, she had hopped out, thinking it a game, then hopped back in again. Jack had tucked the flaps beneath each other, blocking her exit. She mewed, pushed her nose up to the crack of light in the centre. Then a paw. She mewed again, more pathetic this time.

'Here goes,' Jack whispered. 'You'll be happy once you're inside.' He set the food carton on top of the box, then lifted both out of the car, turned to the house and went up the steps. The box felt clumsy in his arms. He put it down in front of the blue door, stood and took a breath. He was regretting already what he had not yet finished doing, missing already the creature that was still right there in front of him. Loretta mewed, a near-silent sound that near enough broke his heart.

Jack wanted to lift Loretta out again, one last time, to hold her and to press his palm to her face, to feel her push back, to rub her cheeks against his hands. But he knew that if he did so she would run, she would spring from his grasp in fear and indignation. He couldn't bear to see her trust shattered like that.

But this would make Vaila happy. He knew that. And surely, after what had happened, Sarah would let the cat stay. It would make her happy, too. It was the right thing to do, he was certain of it.

He leaned forward, rapped hard on the door, then went back down the steps, two at a time, got in the car again and drove away. He felt a tightness in his throat and a pressure behind his eyes. He felt sick. He turned right, towards Treswick, then right again after a mile or so, onto a rough track that ended at a metal gate, where there was just space enough to park. He got out, crossed the gate and walked through the field towards the sea. Sheep looked up from their chewing, assessed the danger, then looked down again. One lamb, fat and sturdy round the shoulders, ran for its mother, plunged its head beneath her to feed and nearly knocked the poor animal to the ground.

The shoreline was fenced off from the field, but Jack aimed for a spot where the wire was sagging, and stepped over to the rough ground beyond. The stones close to the sea were large and uneven, all jagged, awkward shapes. When he was a teenager, Jack's father had taught him how to make and repair walls with the rough rocks of the croft, to mend the holes that would appear over time, rebuilding with the same stones that had been laid there generations before. It was a slow job, a jigsaw without a single solution. One rock went down, then you'd cast an eye over the pile all around you. Which next? That one, with the crust of yolk-yellow lichen on two sides? Or that one, with a smooth face at one end and a broken back at the other. Both would work. Take your pick. Don't think about it too much, though, that's what Sonny always said. Let your hands and your eyes do the thinking. That way things fall into place.

It was something like a song, perhaps, Jack believed. All those choices. A note, a word: each one making space for more. Each one precluding others. Build and build. Let your ears do the thinking.

The walls that Jack had helped maintain in his youth were still standing. They divided and surrounded the smaller fields on the croft. But Young Andrew preferred to replace them with wire fences when damage was done. It was quicker. More secure. And so, when stones tumbled now, when a hole emerged, a new fence would be raised along-side. The walls, one by one, were becoming obsolete.

Maybe old songs were like that, too: made obsolete by new ones. Jack didn't think so, but it was possible. His own songs, which nobody ever heard, well, those were obsolete from the start. He tried then to think of one, to hear it in his head, to comfort himself with music. But he couldn't bring a single melody to mind.

On the beach – if you could give this jumble of stones that name – Jack watched his feet. Each step was a potential fall. His ankles bent one way then another as he navigated towards the water. He took a long stride from one boulder to the next, then short steps on the rocks beyond. Once, not far from here, he had found the chick of a ringed plover, crouching, grey and white and soft and speckled, almost indistinguishable from the stones between which it hid. He had knelt down, peered at it, waiting to see if the bird would move. It had stayed perfectly still.

He heard a lapwing's wiry cry, then, from further up the shore, that thin metallic slide from one note to another, and it put him in mind of a steel guitar. He heard the half-yodel of a curlew's call. He heard the cymbals and insistent applause of the waves.

Jack had always believed, without ever really under-standing what it meant, that the place in which he lived, the landscape he knew, and of which he was in some sense a part, was a landscape of country music. He could not easily put that idea into words, and he could imagine the smirks and laughter of his neighbours if he had ever tried. But he believed it. Truly. He felt the granite and bog and dark waters of these islands to be a part of the same musical geography as the scorched ranchlands of Texas and New Mexico, as the mountains and hollers of Kentucky and Tennessee. Shetland was an ocean away, but what was an ocean, really? It was just another kind of highway.

Jack felt – oh, he couldn't put a name to it, this feeling, but it was like a great gaping hunger. A hole inside, bigger than himself, bigger than this island, bigger than the ocean, bigger than everything. It was contained in him, this hole. And he, in turn was contained in it.

He stepped closer to the waves, the toes of his work boots darkened by the water. He stepped again. It was a shock, the cold, a sharp chisel against his skin. His socks were soaked at once, his ankles flinching. Another step, and then another. The muscles in his legs clenched. Fifteen inches at the bottom of his jeans were wet now, a tideline rising.

The beach was steep as it met the water, and the cold made Jack unsteady. The stones beneath his feet were not solid ground, but ready always to move. He went to take another step – not with any thought or plan, but just because, because, because – and then he slipped. One foot went forward, downward, while his other leg buckled. Jack fell, crumpled, his hands in the sea, his legs in the sea. He landed on his backside, looking out at the horizon. His lungs squeezed inside him and he gasped.

'Pffffaaaw!' he said, out loud. His body juddered.

The waves slapped at Jack's chest. Each one took his breath away. He felt nothing but that awful rhythm, and a shimmering pain from his legs up to his neck. All else was drowned out. It would have been easy to stay where he was, to let the cold have him. It would have been easy to lie back, to close his eyes and surrender his body to the ocean. It would have made perfect sense. To him. Perhaps to others, too.

But he didn't.

Jack dragged himself backwards, still seated, his frozen hands crawling on the rocks beneath him. He turned onto one side, tried to catch his breath, then hauled himself to his feet.

'Christ!' he said, barely able to form a word, he was shivering so hard. 'Christ!'

He stumbled up the slope, onto the grass, not looking back. He found the slack wire and crossed the fence into the field. The sheep observed him again, this lurching buffoon, soaked to the skin. Jack hoped that no one, other than the sheep, could see him now. He hurried towards the gate.

He looked for something dry to sit on in the car, and found an empty plastic bag in the boot. He put it down on the driver's seat and got in. He was still shaking, and it took him a moment to gain the clearness of mind to start the engine, put the heating up and turn the car around. He took it slow. Forward, turn, stop. Reverse, turn, stop. Forward. The car trundled down the track, which seemed more deeply rutted than it had just an hour before. He felt every hole, every stray stone, clunk inside his body.

He turned left onto the main road, and passed no one on his way home. He turned left again at Sarah's house, and an awful thought struck him, that Loretta might still be there, terrified, in her box on the porch. He glanced up at the door, but the box was gone. The cat would be inside the house now. Asleep, most likely. And happy, for sure. She would be curled up on Vaila's bed, perhaps, the girl's hands keeping the kitten company. She'd be purring.

He continued towards home, parked up and got out. He felt stiff now. Sore. A bath was in order. Warm himself up. Loosen his bones. 'Christ,' he said again, 'what a day.' There'd be bruises tomorrow, he knew, he could feel them coming, up his leg, on his left buttock. What was he thinking, paddling about in the sea like that? Could have got himself killed. Could have caught his death. He took his jacket off and hung it up. A drip fell onto the lino. Plup. Then another. Plup. He took his boots off and lifted them. There was a sloshing sound from within.

Jack turned, sopping, to the inside door, and only then noticed the little yellow note stuck to the frosted glass.

*JACK,* the note said, in neat capital letters. *STOP BEING SUCH A BLOODY FOOL!*

Jack did not soak long in the bath. The water turned from too hot to too cold in just a few minutes, and he was out before his skin had even started to pucker. He was thinking, as he lay there, looking up at the polystyrene ceiling tiles, about Sarah's note. Those few stern words, posted on his door, had made him feel both better and worse at once. Better because she had reached out, because she had offered him the chance he thought he had missed. Worse because what little she asked – that he stop hiding away – felt like a lot. Self-recrimination could slip so easily into self-pity. Jack knew this better than anyone.

He put on clean clothes: jeans, a grey jumper. He looked around for something to take with him, a present of some kind, but found nothing. He saw one of the sock mouse toys that Vaila had made, tattered from Loretta's claws and teeth, beneath the coffee table. It wasn't much of a gift, since it had been hers in the first place, but perhaps she'd be glad of it. The kitten would, anyway. He slipped it into his pocket and went outside.

It was a fine early evening, cool but dry, and Jack was surprised by that. For more than a week, Jack had barely noticed the weather at all. He had barely noticed anything.

He dawdled down the track, kicking at the gravel, just as he had on the day of the accident. Only this time without Loretta. It was funny that he missed her already, he thought, after only a few hours. He was pleased that he'd get to see her again now, and he wondered how she'd react. She'd be confused, most likely. Maybe she'd be afraid of him after what he'd done. That thought hurt as soon as it arrived.

He paused in front of Sarah's house, then went up the steps and knocked. He waited a moment, and was about to knock again when she came to the door. She looked exhausted, her eyes fringed with shadows. He felt a thump of compassion and a thump of regret at once.

'Jack,' she said. She neither smiled nor frowned when she saw him, but he thought he noticed her shoulders relax.

'Your cat is still here,' Sarah said. 'She was hiding beneath Vaila's bed last time I saw her, but before that she was peeing on the living-room carpet, which was pretty tiresome, as you can imagine. And I realise you probably thought it would nice for Vaila, but to be honest I don't need anything else to look after at the moment, and I'd really appreciate it if you could just take her away again.'

She looked as though she might be about to cry.

Jack bowed his head. He knew then, as he ought to have known already, that it was not Sarah who had written the note at all. Of course it wasn't. It was Vina. Vina, who knew better than anyone Jack's capacity for self-sabotage, his craven instinct to hide himself away. Vina.

There was a pause of several seconds, a silence as Jack considered what he was going to say. He felt the urge to turn and run, to take the cat and go. But then, almost to his own surprise, he said, 'I've come to see Vaila.'

Sarah nodded before she spoke, and now he was certain: her shoulders really did fall, a contour of strain on her face loosened, just a little. 'It's about time, Jack,' she said, then she stepped aside to let him in.

As he came through the door, stooping slightly, as if he might bang his head on the frame, he felt her hand on his arm.

'She was hurt,' Sarah said quietly, looking at him.

He nodded.

'By you, I mean. Not coming to see her. Not even asking after her. She was hurt. And so was I, frankly. Hurt and annoyed.' Sarah pointed towards the kitchen, and he followed her through the doorway to where the room opened out.

'She'll forgive you,' Sarah went on, 'because that's what she's like. But I wanted you to know, anyway. You let her down.'

Jack spoke towards his feet. 'I thought,' he said, 'I thought that you would blame me. I thought because—'

'Because of the flowers,' Sarah said. 'You thought I'd blame you because of the flowers. I understand. And you can understand, too, why I've been furious with myself, since it was my earphones she was wearing. Which I lent her. Which is why she didn't hear the car.'

Jack had forgotten about the earphones.

'But none of that matters, does it?' Sarah was still whispering, which somehow made her words all the more painful.

'We can both blame ourselves all we like, but it doesn't change anything. Because Vaila doesn't blame us. Not for what happened. She just doesn't understand why her friend, who lives next door, hasn't been to see her. Why he left his cat at the front door and ran away, for goodness' sake! I mean, what were you thinking?'

Jack knew it would take him a long time to explain himself to Sarah. And perhaps he would never manage to do so. But he felt, too – and this, *this* was a surprise – he felt an urge to try. Not to make excuses or to shirk the blame for what he had and had not done, but just to explain himself, to tell Sarah how this, how all of this, had happened.

There would be time for that, he hoped. It was not too late.

Sarah led him down the hallway to a room on the right, painted pale blue, like a blackbird's egg. On the bed in the far corner, Vaila was sitting up, her hands folded in front of her on the duvet. The cast on her left arm seemed too large for her body. She looked at Jack and grinned.

There is always a day in summer, in Shetland, when all the creatures of the place – the birds, the livestock, the people – seem to realise together that the season is tilting towards its end. An urgency sweeps over the islands then, a clamour of making-the-most-of-it. In a place with so few trees (and there were none at all in the near vicinity of Hamar), autumn can be less like a full season and more like a short, steep slope. There may be days of fine weather still to come, maybe weeks if luck will have it, but once you reach that slope, once the year leans towards winter, it is hard to forget the fact. And so, when that tipping point comes – often as early as the second week in August – minds turn to what still needs to be done. Chicks are fed and fattened and hurried from their nests. Lambs are nudged towards an independence that few of them will ever need. A sharpness taints the air, and the sunsets, when they come, can be glorious. Outrageous, even.

Such a sunset arrived that very evening, bathing the islands in a light as thick as syrup and as bright as salmon flesh. Everything strained towards that light. Even the sheep – so often oblivious or indifferent – turned their faces to the west, staring in shared silence at the day's end, bewitched.

Inside the house at Hamar, in the shadow of the ridge that gave the place its name, the radiance that fell upon the islands went unnoticed. Jack Paton, who had returned from his next-door neighbour's house an hour before, and who had drunk a very large glass of bourbon since then, was in a buoyant mood. Relieved, cheerful – exuberant, even. He had turned the music up so loud in the living room that it had drowned out everything else. The world outside lay beyond his attention.

Jack was holding his drink in one hand, and with the other was tapping his knee in time with the music. Charley Pride. What a voice that man had! What a comfortable, comforting voice. Top five, Jack thought. Definitely top five.

He tried to formulate a list then, but he couldn't keep it still.

George Jones, naturally.

Emmylou Harris, certainly.

Charley Pride, undoubtedly.

But then?

Well, then there was Patsy Cline, Merle Haggard, Tammy Wynette, Marty Robbins, Patty Loveless, Don Williams, Conway Twitty, Dolly Parton, Ray Price, George Strait. There was Loretta.

And then . . .

Jack thought of other voices, more weary and hard-worn. Voices that could muster the marvellous as if out of nowhere. He thought of voices torn apart by time or by tobacco. He thought of the way a voice could break, how it could crack under the weight of itself and all that it remembered. He thought of what could flourish in those cracks, what could spring to life in the most meagre of places.

He thought of Kris Kristofferson, Johnny Cash, John Prine, Steve Earle, Lucinda Williams, Guy Clark, Ralph Stanley, Townes Van Zandt: a ragged and glorious choir.

What was a voice really for? Jack asked himself. What could one do that another could not? Was there such a thing as a perfect voice?

The questions, that night, kept coming.

How did a melody work? How many lives could one song have? How much sadness could be carried in a single line?

Ach, Jack, what in the hell are you on about?

His head swirled in the slow current of the whiskey. He took another swig, then reached, once again, for his guitar – that beautiful old Martin – and the kitten, curled up on the sofa, with its tail wrapped like a scarf around itself, lifted one eyelid to watch.

# THE ATLANTIC WALTZ

I was waltzing on the waves
I was foolish, I was brave
I was doing the best I could do that I could
when
I let down my guard, the sea hit me hard
And it took me like a piece of
~~spun~~
                            driftwood

### Chorus

(It'll rock you, it'll roll you)
(It'll try to control you)                    soon?
(It'll toss you and turn you, till one day
  you learn to keep time with this
  rhythm of salt    ~~you are~~ nobody's fault)

That beautiful Atlantic Waltz.


Like a ~~fading~~ wilting wallflower ~~that after~~
 In the night's final hour
~~I have watched this old dance from~~
                    endless?                        after
On the edge of this ancient dance floor

Too late I stepped in & I started to spin
        lost?
 I was swallowed and spat out once more

### CHORUS

# the ocean wild and wide

## 1981

'Canna keep the bloody woman awa,' Sonny said, from behind his newspaper. 'Every time we turn aroond, there she is!'

Kathleen laughed and set the kettle on the Rayburn. Her husband's exaggeration amused her. Queen Elizabeth was coming back for the third time, that was all. She had been there in the islands on the day Jack was born, and then again the year that Tom died. This time she was coming to open, officially, the Sullom Voe oil terminal.

'You ken he was in Sooth Georgia when I was there, too?' Sonny said. 'Philip. The husband. Een of the seasons I was there. Fifty-seven, I think.'

Kathleen did know this. It had been mentioned often over the years.

'What does she need to open it for, onyway?' Sonny went on. 'There's been oil flowin for twa years. What difference will cuttin a ribbon make?' He folded his *Shetland Times* and laid it on the table, a look of disappointment on his face.

Kathleen knew it wasn't the Queen that was bothering him. Jack had been gone just over a week, and both of them missed him. They worried. If she'd asked, Sonny would have shaken his head. Ach, he'll be fine, he would have told her. And probably he believed it. But that didn't mean he wasn't worried, too. Jack's parents found it hard to imagine him living in the city. And not just because neither of them had ever been to Glasgow.

Jack's decision to go – inexplicable to them – might have seemed less strange, less concerning, if he'd been able to articulate any reason for the move. If he'd told them a plan, even an idea. But there was nothing. One day he seemed content with his job and his life, the next he was buying a ticket to leave.

The house was quiet. Kathleen missed the sound of Jack's guitar, muffled behind his bedroom door. She missed the sound of his voice, singing, the melodies she recognised and those she did not. Some of them, she knew, Jack had written himself – she had heard him trying things out, over and over – though when she'd asked him to play one for her he'd just shaken his head. Her beautiful boy, across the sea, was never not on her mind. Time passed more slowly with Jack gone. The hours crawled.

When the day came, a fortnight later, for the official opening, the royal visit, Sonny woke up cheerful. 'Let's take a trip,' he said as they ate breakfast together. 'Let's go oot in the boat.'

Kathleen glanced through the kitchen window. It was dull and grey: hardly the weather for an outing. But she nodded. They were spending more time together now, she and Sonny, and they were enjoying that time as well. They had settled into their marriage in the past year or two; that's how it seemed to her. It was as if, growing older, they had become more comfortably themselves, alone and with each other. The sound of Sonny returning home each evening came, to Kathleen, like a sigh of relief.

But still, Sonny rarely took her out on the sea – it was his place, not hers – and so she felt glad of this invitation. She would make lunch, she said, and a flask of tea to bring with them.

The *Wayfarer* was tied up by the pier at Treswick, and because the tide was low they had to clamber down the steel ladder to get on board. Kathleen had the bag with food and drink, and Sonny followed with the canister of petrol. He topped up the outboard motor, primed it, unfastened the boat from the pier, then started the engine. It caught first time, and Sonny winked at Kathleen. 'Gettin the knack for this,' he yelled over the roar of the outboard.

They chugged away from the pier, away from the village, and turned north, in the direction of Hamar. Gulls wheeled above them, then moved on. The sea was close to calm, with only a slow swell from the southwest, rising, falling, as the little boat went on its way.

Kathleen was wearing two woollen jumpers, a coat and a set of oilskins, and still she wasn't warm. But sitting in the bow, facing forward, with the cold air on her cheeks, she felt happy for the first time since Jack had left. She closed her eyes, let the motion of the boat move her body. She pulled the sleeves of a jumper down over her fingers.

Sonny, in the stern, was happy, too. Always, being out on the water felt like coming home.

There was nowhere in particular they were going that day. On his own, Sonny would usually fish, but today they would find a place to stop, to pull the boat out and eat their lunch. There was a beach just a little further along this shore. It was stony, not easy to get the boat up, but it would do. Or else, perhaps, he could just switch off the engine and let them drift a while.

Sonny slowed as they approached the land closest to the house. They couldn't see it, of course – the high ridge blocked their view of everything beyond – but both of them turned to look. Seeing the place from this angle never got old. There was always something Sonny hadn't noticed before.

He cut the motor.

Kathleen turned back to check that everything was okay, and he nodded. 'Just lookin,' he said. 'Just lookin.'

Twenty miles away, as the fulmar flew, Queen Elizabeth was preparing to speak, to celebrate the oil from beneath the ocean and the money that came with it. You could almost hear it, that money, clinking into the islands' coffers like wind chimes in a gale. A brass band began to play.

Sonny, not thinking then of such things at all, moved from the stern to the centre thwart of the boat, and lifted the oars into the rowlocks. 'The engine's too lood,' he said.

As he started to row, his back to his wife, Sonny's voice rose up, quiet at first, then more confident as he found the melody. He was singing between oar strokes, in time with the boat.

*I'll take you home again, Kathleen*
*Across the ocean wild and wide*
*To where your heart has ever been*
*Since first you were my bonnie bride.*

Behind him, beneath the pale sky, his wife was smiling, her arms wrapped around herself. She always loved it when he sang that song. It could ease any hurt in her.

*Oh, I will take you back, Kathleen*
*To where your heart will feel no pain*
*And when the fields are fresh and green*
*I'll take you to your home, Kathleen.*

Sonny tried to whistle, as Slim Whitman had, but he couldn't do it, and broke down laughing instead. The pair of them, husband and wife for more than twenty years now, laughed together in the boat.

And then, a shadow. A darkness in the water.

Both of them, Sonny and Kathleen, looked up in the same instant, as if their heads had been tugged by puppet strings. But the source of the shadow was not above them.

The moment of understanding was slow. It came through murk and confusion, until it could not be denied any longer. Beneath the boat, and rising, was the grey wizened skin of a whale.

There was a bump as its body met the keel, and there was a pause just long enough for them to hope that a bump was the worst that would happen. But the whale kept coming, ascending, with the boat upon its back. Somehow, it didn't tip – not yet – but seemed to balance on the animal, like a tossed coin landing on its edge.

Kathleen's terrified eyes were on her husband, as if he could do something, anything, to stop this. But Sonny knew that he could not. He knew that they were trapped, the pair of them, in a moment of equilibrium that would not, could not, last.

And as they teetered there, atop the beast, Sonny, who had turned in his seat, let go of the oars in his hands. He looked at his wife then, and he began again to sing.

*And when the fields are fresh and green . . .*

Sonny held the note, just as Slim had done, clinging to it like something living, something wild, something with an urge towards freedom.

*I'll take you to your home . . .*

The boat shifted on the fulcrum of the whale's back. It leaned, tipped, then toppled, slipping and tumbling towards the water. As it fell, Sonny and Kathleen reached for each other, as if their love were a kind of safety. As if that old, old hunger could keep them afloat.

The whale turned, it rolled, its back a broad expanse of burnished stone. A mountain. A desert. And then the tail: carved around the edges, raised like a banner of victory or commemoration. The flukes stood upright – a miracle – for second after second, until

as silent as it first emerged
the great whale
slipped back
into the
wide
ocean
blue.

# Acknowledgements

From the early eighteenth century until 1963, when the industry ended – for Britain, at least – a disproportionate number of Atlantic whalers came from Shetland. I first met former whalers there when I was still a boy, and to me their stories were both thrilling and horrifying at once. While writing this book, I was grateful for the many recollections gathered in *Shetland's Whalers Remember*, compiled and published by Gibbie Fraser. I also referred to R.B. Robertson's *Of Whales and Men*, which I borrowed from Steven Laurenson many years ago, then 'forgot' to return. Sandy Winterbottom's *The Two-Headed Whale* was published as I was writing this book, and I greatly appreciated her humane account of the life and death of a young Scottish whaler, and the complicated legacies of this industry.

One of the joys of working on this particular novel was exploring the music that lies at its heart. Duncan McLean provided numerous listening suggestions when I was just

starting out, and his excellent book *Lone Star Swing* offered many more.

Andrew Gifford, Jenna Reid and Laura-Beth Salter helped me to bring Jack's songs to life, and I can't thank them enough for that.

'My Old Cottage Home', sung by The Carter Family and many others, was written in 1880 by Robert A. Glenn.

'I'll Take You Home Again, Kathleen', sung by Slim Whitman and many others, was written in 1875 by Thomas P. Westendorf.

I'm hugely grateful to Mary Blance and Lyndsie Bourgon, who read drafts of this novel and offered comments and corrections on some of the historical detail. Any mistakes that made it through are mine alone. Silas House read a later draft and generously reassured me that I'd not got country music all wrong.

Jenny Brown is the best agent anyone could hope for, and I'm thankful, always, for her enthusiasm and hard work. Thanks to Leah Woodburn, who made the process of editing this book a real pleasure. Thanks also to Ed Wall, to Rali Chorbadzhiyska, Leila Cruickshank, Anna Frame, Jamie Norman and the rest of the amazing team at Canongate.

Thanks most of all to Roxani Krystalli. Everything – this book included – is made better by her.